# THE LOST DISPATCH

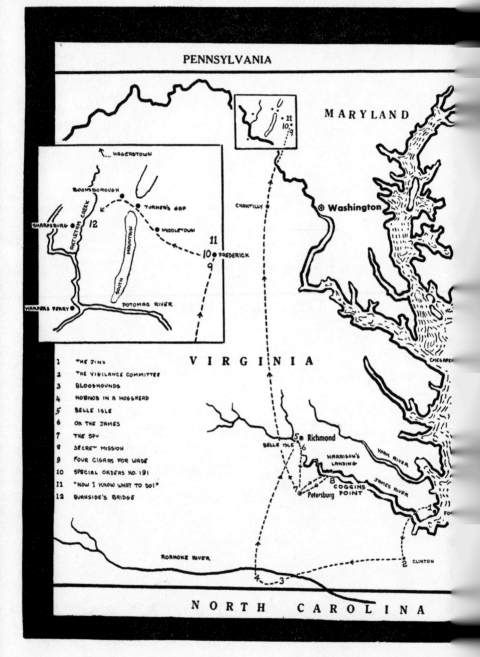

# THE LOST
# DISPATCH

## A STORY OF ANTIETAM

*DONALD J. SOBOL*

*CHAPTER DECORATIONS
BY ANTHONY PALUMBO*

**FRANKLIN WATTS**
575 Lexington Avenue, New York 22, N.Y.

*Second Printing*

**Library of Congress Catalog Card Number: 58-9786**

*For*
*Maurice Tiplitz*
*and to the memory of*
*Lillian Himoff Tiplitz*

# AUTHOR'S NOTE

On September 13, 1862, a dispatch was found in a meadow outside Frederick, Maryland. Its finding changed the course of the Civil War.

While many authorities have come to agree on how the dispatch was found, no one knows to this day how it was lost. On this riddle *The Lost Dispatch* is based. The plot adheres to fact where fact is confirmable.

Because the book is a work of fiction and not a history, bibliography, footnotes, and appendixes have been excluded. Nevertheless, the author wishes to express his indebtedness to the following persons who have assisted him and in many cases provided data which he had not been able to locate on his own: Dr. Helen Lane of New Haven, Connecticut; G. Gleen Clift of the Kentucky Historical Society; Amelia Hogencamp of the Indiana State Library; J. W. Doswell of the *Suffolk News-Herald,* Suffolk, Virginia; David C. Mearns and Henry J. Dubester of the Library of Congress; H. G. Jones of the State of North Carolina Department of Archives and History; Guy Coulombe of Staten Island, New York, a fellow member of the Civil War Round of New York; Moritia-Leah Frederick of the Donnell Library, New York Public Library, New York; Robert A. Lively of Princeton University, Princeton, New Jersey; and James I. Robertson, Jr., of Emory University, Atlanta, Georgia.

— *The author*

# Contents

"I do not know who lost the dispatch . . . I went into Maryland to give battle, and could I have kept General McClellan in ignorance of my position and plans a day or two longer, I would have fought and crushed him."

        — *Robert E. Lee*
        Washington College
        Lexington, Virginia
        Feb. 15, 1868

# THE LOST DISPATCH

*Chapter 1*

# The Jinx

From the encampment of the Fifty-sixth Kentucky
Volunteers the smoke of a hundred breakfast fires twisted
up into the March sky. Sergeant Wade Baxter was accus-
tomed to campfires, and he sat outwardly composed. But
his hands were clenched tight on his rifle and mess gear,
and he watched the black columns rising with desperate
concentration.

Having filled his stomach, the trick was now to find something to fill his mind. Nothing he'd read, and nothing in his
year's experience in the Union army, had prepared him for
the mysterious shootings of the past week.

He shook himself. If he thought about the shootings, he'd
never have the nerve to inspect the men on picket duty.

1

So he concentrated on the smoke, aware that the men around his campfire were observing him in guarded, sidelong glances. A whistle blew; a cook was about to dump a coffee kettle. Several men, cup in hand, dashed for the mess tent. None, however, stirred from the fire where Wade sat.

Uncomfortably Wade looked at his watch — ten to six. He peered at the smoke another five minutes and then got up. The slight effort to balance his plate and rifle strained his careful pose of indifference.

Around him eyes lifted with sullen fear. The clatter of tin plates ceased. In the silence, a snapple-pop from the flaming logs burst with startling loudness.

Wade moved from the campfire as though nothing were wrong. In his gait was that rangy sleepiness he often used — when little was happening — and which some mistook for the woolgathering of youth.

He continued on through the rows of tents and stopped at an icy creek about half a mile beyond. A frail, tattered Negro boy appeared suddenly from a thicket like a soft, upward stroke of the mother earth.

Wade held out his plate with its cleanly trimmed savings of food.

Wordlessly the boy stepped forward. His arm snaked out. Salt meat and hardtack vanished behind a white blockade of teeth.

The boy, a mute, was easy prey for the bigger children in the rough scramble around the army garbage pails. Wade had befriended him and these morning meetings had become ritual.

The boy turned to go, grinning his thanks.

"Gilliam," Wade called to him.

Gilliam stopped with a look of grave inquiry.

"Will you do something for me?"

The boy nodded, and Wade said, "You know the wood —
the one our pickets face. Go out there and hide yourself. If
you hear a rifle fired from the trees, try to get a look at whoever did the shooting. But don't take any chances, understand?"

Gilliam drew himself erect, excited by this opportunity
of repaying the tall young soldier. He saluted and scam-
pered off.

Wade was on the verge of calling him back. Instead, he
scooped a handful of gravelly sand and scoured his mess
gear. He rubbed slowly, ashamed of drawing Gilliam into
his nightmare.

He told himself that Gilliam would be outside the danger. Besides, there wasn't going to be any shooting. None
of the pickets had been killed when other sergeants inspected them. And if he believed he alone attracted enemy
fire, then he believed the evil, frightening thing the men
were whispering.

He cleared the whispers from his mind. Hanging his
mess gear to dry by his tent, he started the long walk down
the road toward the pickets.

A long and lonely walk. Wade heard the hush which
moved through the ranks apace of him.

And twice he heard, or thought he heard, someone snarl,
"*Jinx!*"

The name burned like a saber cut. Wade flinched, and
once past a straggly fringe of pines quickly left the road.
He sucked in a steadying breath.

In front of him the pickets lolled in groups of twos and

threes. Rifles were laid by in garrison unconcern. For months there had been no major action in this part of Virginia, the peninsula formed by the York and James rivers. The men regarded picket duty as an irksome, unnecessary precaution. The lazy ones drowsed, the bellyachers swapped complaints, the homesick reread their letters. Wade, approaching from behind, had not been noticed.

Two hundred yards beyond the pickets, in Confederate territory, lay the dense wood into which he had dispatched Gilliam.

Wade stared at the trees. "Don't let it happen again," he prayed.

The wood crouched like an eyeless monster, glowering back at him through the sockets of a million dark recesses, a million ambushes. In the past week it had sprung to life three times, spitting fire. The score: three Yank sentries killed, and each, fantastically, by Wade's side. The wood seemed to lie in wait just for him.

A cough sounded too noisily. A warning shout followed. The pickets seized their rifles. Wade had been seen.

He began the inspection. He walked rapidly, though conscious of appearing not to hurry. As he reached the middle of the line he realized he was counting the men still to be inspected. Fourteen . . . thirteen . . .

"Abe's hat."

The sentry who had spoken the password smiled drunkenly. "Slow down, lad," he muttered. "Ain't nothin' goin' tuh happen."

"Of course nothing is going to happen," Wade said, smelling the source of the other's boldness.

The sentry belched and lifted his rifle. "You take a peek

and see if Billy McNeil keeps his rifle clean. You show 'em you ain't scairt. I ain't."

Aware of making a beautiful, stationary target, Wade accepted the rifle, examined it, and thrust it back at chest height. "C-clean," he stammered.

"Now that there's an inspection," the sentry said, "you ain't no jinx, lad. Ain't nothin' tuh be scairt — "

The sentence finished in a stream of blood. Wade heard the rifle blast a second after he saw the sentry's jaw split apart. He reached out, but the stricken man pitched sideways from his grasp and lay lifeless.

*You ain't no jinx.* The words seemed to echo up from the bloody sack at Wade's feet, mocking him.

He recoiled. He spun and raced for the wood, impelled by a single, burning notion. He had to capture that Reb sharpshooter, had to show him to be an ordinary human. If the men of the Fifty-sixth saw a prisoner of flesh and bone, they might discard the superstition of a jinx.

He searched frantically, snagging his rifle on branches and tearing his uniform. He saw no one. After ten minutes of running, his legs were trembling and his heart slammed against his ribs like a wet, caged thing. He flopped upon the ground, exhausted.

A footstep crunched behind him. Wade squirmed around on his belly and threw the rifle to his shoulder. His sights trained on the small, dark figure of Gilliam.

Wade jumped to his feet and, despite his impatience, questioned the frightened boy calmly. Gilliam had seen the sharpshooter, and motioning Wade to follow, led him to a spot from which the picket line was visible.

Wade examined the ground. It was scuffed by hoof

marks. The Reb, then, had been mounted, and all hope of overtaking him was lost.

Gilliam had more to communicate. He hopped about and fenced with an imaginary saber. Was the Reb an officer? Gilliam nodded his head, "Yes." Of what rank the boy did not know.

For a moment that seemed the sum of it.

Suddenly Gilliam's face brightened. He held up his left hand, keeping the last two fingers curled into the palm.

"He had only three fingers on that hand?"

The boy gestured triumphantly.

"Good work, soldier," declared Wade, pretending the missing fingers were the solution instead of a clue. "*Dismissed!*"

The little scout, relieved of military duty, executed one of his better salutes and skipped off for an afternoon of oystering. For Wade, the episode remained ominously incomplete. The "jinx" had claimed a fourth victim, and turning heavily toward camp, he imagined the reception awaiting him.

When he emerged from the wood, the pickets were standing at their posts. The dead sentry was being lifted upon a litter, surrounded by a dozen soldiers. Dozens more swarmed from the camp.

At the appearance of Wade the forefront of the mob halted. Those in the rear closed rapidly, till a wall of bluecoats, thickened steadily by newcomers, barred his path.

Wade acted instinctively. Opposite him ranged half the regiment, a mob inflamed by the poison of superstition. They could deluge him at any instant; only someone to assume command was needed. Wade searched for that someone.

A great, pugnacious bear of a private whom the men called Dutch seemed a likely candidate. Ringleader or not, he was indisputably the biggest and meanest man in the Fifty-sixth.

Before the mob had organized into collective action, Wade curled his hands around his lips. "I want you, Dutch!" he shouted. All trace of sleepiness had left his gait as he strode for the big man.

The challenge to individual combat took the mob by surprise. The men wavered, disconcerted by the appeal to fair play.

"Hell, Dutch'll chew him alive!" a voice cried.

The cry settled the issue. The convenience of letting someone else do the dirty work prevailed, and the men formed an arena. Those nearest Dutch encouraged him with gory images of the Jinx, dashed and impotent.

Dutch squinted about him in suspicion. The lightning change in his status from bully to champion at first baffled, then pleased and assured him.

"Take off them stripes, mountain boy," he bellowed.

Wade stopped and very deliberately peeled off his shirt. By so doing he waived all privileges of rank. Bare to the waist, sergeant faced private, even up.

There was a dead pause. Dutch shrugged his massive shoulders meaningfully, sampling their readiness for the job to be done. Around the knuckles of his right hand he had wrapped a handkerchief.

"Yeh ready, Jinx?"

"I'm ready."

Dutch advanced, gliding on his toes with unexpected, sinister grace. He feinted Wade off balance and cuffed him wickedly on the side of the head. Wade staggered but did not fall, and Dutch retreated, smiling and immensely confident.

The men cheered. They had feared a fast ending which would cheat them. The Jinx could take a blow. Good! Let him stand up and suffer.

Dutch satisfied the most bloodthirsty. He fought with practiced skill. He punished Wade and bled him, systematically withholding the mercy of a knockout. Occasionally someone called to stop it. Several officers joined the mob, but seeing the participants, did not intervene. Four dead comrades demanded justice of any kind.

Wade fought as long as he could lift his arms. Once he hit Dutch's nose savagely and knew he'd broken it. Enraged, growling in pain, Dutch smashed blows in wild fury. Wade stumbled into him blindly, groping for a hold and meeting the hard resistance of the ground, and the inky billows of unconsciousness.

He awoke to a body that was his and yet too numbed to do his bidding. He lay on his bunk, washed and naked. Tom Watson, his tent mate, sat beside him.

"How do you feel?" Tom inquired anxiously.

"Like I've paid my debt," replied Wade.

"Why didn't you quit?" Tom reproved. "You big, stupid ox."

Wade tried to get up, but contented himself with rolling on his side. "Dutch?"

"He won't look the same, ever," Tom said pleasantly.

His tone changed. "You know, Wade, there's a pattern to these deaths. I've developed a theory about that sharpshooter — "

"Sharpshooter*s*," corrected Wade. "There have been four deaths."

"Four deaths, all right," agreed Tom, "and *one* sharpshooter, my theory says. The *same* Reb killed all four of our pickets."

Wade snorted and picked up an illustrated weekly from beside the bunk. The friends had always refrained from discussing Wade's strange influence on the deaths of the sentries. Now more than ever he wanted to leave the subject alone.

But Tom persisted. "Did you ever think it might be more than an eerie coincidence that you were standing beside every sentry who was killed?" He jerked the paper from Wade's grasp. "This theory," he exclaimed, "may sound crazy to you. You've got to listen, though. It's — "

A soldier stuck his head into the tent. "Sergeant Baxter? Colonel Winslow wants to see you right away."

Wade mumbled and edged painfully off the bunk. Tom had to help him into his uniform. He refused further assistance, and by the time he reached Colonel Winslow's tent he'd walked off some of the aching stiffness.

"You sent for me, sir?"

Colonel Winslow, seated at his desk, motioned Wade into a wicker chair.

"My brother, Colonel Robert Winslow, is with Grant in Tennessee. I want you to take this message to him," the colonel said. While he spoke, he scribbled on a piece of brown wrapping paper. "Have you an envelope, Sergeant?"

Astonished, Wade fumbled in his pocket. He produced
a batch of his Aunt Mae's letters and passed an envelope
to the colonel.

"Good," the colonel grunted, slipping the brown paper
into the rumpled envelope. "Here — not strictly according
to regulation, but just as well. If you lose it, nobody will
think it much important."

"I won't lose it, sir."

The colonel shifted in his chair like a teacher who has
before him a dull pupil. "Your route will take you back
to Kentucky. I expect you'll want to stop off and see your
folks."

"My folks are dead, sir. I live with my Aunt Mae."

"Well, you'll want to see her. You'll need civilian clothes,
of course. I've informed the sutler, and he has some for
you. I don't wish every Reb hothead in Virginia popping
at the blue uniform as you go by." He opened a drawer.
"Here's money — it's yours, two months' pay in advance.
I'll see to a horse. Any questions, sergeant?"

"None, sir."

"Then we understand each other?" The colonel rose
and for the first time met Wade's gaze. "Good luck."

"Thank you, sir."

Outside, Wade felt a blaze of resentment and helpless-
ness. He walked in a bitter trance, telling himself the
colonel had no alternative. The men wouldn't eat or sleep
or march near him once they got to campaigning.

This way it was all very legal. No embarrassing investi-
gations. No transfer to another unit. And, of course, no
word of a jinx. A colonel in the United States Army dared
not even pooh-pooh superstition, or left-handedly concede

its presence. The army was run by plan and reason, not by witchcraft.

Wade slipped the message into his pocket. So that was that. He was to carry a message which might be conveniently lost — indeed, was expected to be lost. And what if he overstayed his leave at home? He might never catch up with the Fifty-sixth. How Colonel Winslow would appreciate that!

He allowed himself a bit of malicious pleasure, envisioning the colonel's dilemma in juggling his service record. The first part handled easily: Wade Daniel Baxter, age 16, enlisted Louisa, Lawrence County, Kentucky, March 7, 1861; promoted sergeant, Big Bethel, Virginia, June 10, 1861; *March 18, 1862* — discharged? . . . captured? . . . killed? . . . what?

At the sutler's log hut Wade asked about the clothing. The sutler, a private merchant licensed by the army, brought forth a carpetbag. Packed inside was a complete outfit: Nankeen trousers, black broadcloth frock coat, linen shirt, and black cravat. Wade purchased the lot (at half their worth), plus a light tan slouch hat.

The colonel did less handsomely in providing transportation. The horse tethered outside Wade's tent stood spread-legged under the full cavalry rig, neck drooping dully in the midmorning sun.

Wade patted the lusterless black coat. "Nobody wants you, eh, old boy? Nobody wants me, either, so I guess we'll get along fine. A pair of outcasts, that's us. Outcast . . . how'd you like that for a name?"

Outcast it was, and Wade got busy trimming him of unneeded baggage. The horse confronted a journey across two hundred and fifty miles of Rebel country to the mountains of Kentucky. For that, every surplus ounce had to be stripped from his back.

In the saddlebags Wade kept rations, underclothing, socks, an iron picket pin, and a lariat. He lengthened the hooded stirrups, checked the canteen, and tightened the slicker-encased blanket roll. From two heavy boxes he removed a few extra rounds of cartridges and percussion caps and shoved them into the twin pistol holsters up front.

The rest of the equipment he carried into the tent. Then he donned his fancy civilian attire and sat down to wait for Tom Watson. Tom alone in the regiment would not applaud his departure, and Wade wanted to bid him farewell.

Time dragged without sign of his friend. When at last Tom strolled into the tent, night had fallen and Wade's temper had shortened.

"Where the dickens have you been?" he demanded.

"Letting it get dark," replied Tom. "I figured you'd wait to say good-by. I couldn't allow you to ride out of camp in broad daylight."

"I'm not afraid of the boys seeing me."

"That's it. You're not afraid of anything."

Tom's slight, youthful appearance made his keenness all the more unexpected, and his deductions often downright startling. Wade was startled now.

"How did you know I was leaving?"

"The horse outside, for one thing," answered Tom. "Everything fits beautifully."

"Fits what?"

"My theory. You wouldn't have got ten miles in broad daylight."

"Who's to stop me?"

"Oh, good heavens, you numskull!" wailed Tom in exasperation. "The sharpshooter. The devil of a sharpshooter, that's who!"

Wade laughed scoffingly.

"Believe in the idiotic superstition of a jinx if you prefer!"

"I can't do that," Wade muttered.

"Then you'd better listen," retorted Tom. "Because if you go prancing out of camp, riding high and defiant, you'll stop a bullet."

Wade settled tensely on the bunk. In spite of an impulse to poke fun, he felt vaguely disturbed. Something in Tom's words suggested a truth faintly sensed, a concept tantalizingly beyond his grasp.

"All right," Wade said uneasily. "What's your theory?"

Tom began pacing the floor. "Let's suppose there is a man who vitally wants something you have — perhaps something you know or carry on your person. He has this problem: how to get that something while you walk safely in the middle of an army."

"Why doesn't he just come up and ask for it?"

"Obviously, that's the one thing he can't do — and that indicates he's in a Reb uniform," Tom replied. "Now to solve his problem, let's endow our man with dead-eye marksmanship and a cold-blooded willingness to kill. From any of a dozen hills he watches you through field glasses — watches you drill, sleep, eat, and play. He watches

you inspect the pickets, and he gets an inspiration. Kill the
sentry standing next to you and — "

"Make me look like a jinx!" gasped Wade.

"Precisely. And how well it's worked! Tonight he'll have
you all to himself out there."

Wade felt again the impulse to scoff. The theory was
utterly preposterous — one man cunning enough to control a regiment from afar! Yet Wade sat rooted, peering
into the triangle of night exposed by the open tent flap,
fascinated by the idea of such a foe.

"Three fingers on the left hand," Wade muttered to himself. Out loud, he said, "I'm not carrying any secret doc-
uments, and I don't know anything special. So what does
this fellow want of *me*?"

The thuds of Tom's footfalls died on the planks. He
turned slightly, in a curious way that seemed more a shud-
der. "Don't you see it? There's only one thing he could be
after — your body."

"My *what*? T-that's insane!"

"Maybe it is," asserted Tom softly. "Maybe he's a mad-
man. We can find out. I'll ride a piece with you tonight,
about a mile behind. If he picks up your trail, we'll have
him nicely between us."

Wade hesitated, overcome by bewilderment and out-
rage. Finally, he said, "It's a deal," and held out his hand.
Tom reached for it unwittingly. The fingers clenched, and
struck. Tom fell without an outcry.

Swiftly Wade unhitched Outcast and climbed into the
saddle. The danger — if it did exist — was his, not Tom's.
He dug back his heels. Outcast whinnied in protest, but
soon was out beyond the protective rim of the picket line,

galloping across the vast and slumbering lids of Virginia.

In that first mile, where danger pressed hardest, Wade relied upon night to blur his identity, and then, if failing to outwhisk pursuit, planned to outmaneuver it.

Leaning forward in the saddle, he flattened himself into a low silhouette. The road curved and pitched. Holes and wagon ruts flew under him in ceaseless bombardment. So concerned was he with sustaining the early pace at all hazard that the bordering, tree-banked hills stroked by unnoticed.

It made no difference. Had he contemplated the woods with the patient, midnight eye of an owl, he could not have detected the tall figure standing deep among the pines.

As Wade swept past on the road below, the watching man lowered his field glasses and silently lifted himself upon his horse.

## Chapter 2

# The Vigilance Committee

A MILE RACED BY, AND THEN ANOTHER. WITH EVERY PASSING second Wade expected to hear the shrill whine of a bullet reaching for him. Farther and farther from the Union camps he sped, body cramped low and cheek laid by Outcast's plunging neck. But no rifle blast pierced the clenching stillness, no bullet singled him out. Night rested softly upon a land seemingly asleep and harmless.

At length he shifted up into the saddle and stole a rearward glance. The road behind lay straight for several hundred yards, and empty. He slowed Outcast to a trot, musing indignantly on Tom Watson's theory. Mysterious sharpshooter — in a pig's ear!

Believing himself absolutely safe, he remained seated

16

upright in the saddle. After crossing the James River on an old flatboat, he headed due west for Kentucky. A spring rain began to fall, and he dismounted to unstrap the slicker.

As his weight dropped upon one foot, the realization of why he had ridden this far unscathed darted through his mind.

A skilled marksman makes sure of his first shot, or does not shoot. Darkness and now rain made a galloping target too difficult to bring down. Far from being a daydream, Three-Fingers might well be all too real — a marksman who was biding his time and picking his spot.

Wade remounted speedily. After about a quarter mile he found what he needed: a sharp curve and just beyond it an overhead branch vaulting the road. Standing on the saddle, he grasped the branch and kicked Outcast forward.

The branch bent. Wade jiggled and tossed. Wood snapped in a series of rasping discords, tumbling him. He bounced up mud-caked but satisfied.

The branch dangled vertically. The smaller limbs, growing at the tip, formed a broomlike obstruction close to the ground. If not an impassable barrier, they served at least as a means of checking a pursuer momentarily.

A moment was all Wade required. He led Outcast into the neighboring trees and tethered him. Withdrawing the ponderous twin cavalry pistols, he slipped back to a point where he might observe his snare while retaining cover.

For nearly ten minutes raindrops made the only motion, the only noise, as they dug murmurously into the earth. Wet, cold, impatient, Wade began doubting again. He cursed himself for a fool. The sharpshooter existed all right — in Tom Watson's imagination!

He rose from his haunches, and immediately ducked back. The slap-rustle of harness and mane had sounded faintly. Down the road a horse shook water from its neck.

Presently horse and rider loomed round the bend, traveling at a leisurely walk. Wade's fingers relaxed on the pistols. He had no quarrel with a stray Reb who obviously was pursuing nothing more than his own easy way.

"An ordinary Reb," thought Wade. And in the next instant the rider proved himself anything but ordinary.

He read the meaning of the broken branch with the swiftness of instinct. Letting out a fiendish Rebel yell, he veered his mount wide and hurtled past.

Wade scrambled onto the road, marveling. The Reb had evaded him in a spurt of dazzling horsemanship. The snare had caught only a cap.

The cap bore neither mark nor name, and Wade stuffed it in a saddlebag, crumpling it fiercely. He cantered back the way he'd come and, reaching a crossroad, heeled Outcast in a new route toward the southwest. If the Reb had been the mysterious Three-Fingers, accounts were squared. Each had eluded the other.

Yet the memory of that shadowy form, warlike as a bayonet thrust and as deadly quick, haunted Wade. And there was something else about the Reb . . . something hazy and frightening. All through the night Wade tried to recall what it was. Not until dawn flickered in the east did he succeed.

The Reb had been walking his horse as if he had all the time in the world to pick an ambush, as if he knew he could not lose his quarry.

*"But that,"* thought Wade, *"can only be if he knows my exact destination."*

Nervously he shook the reins. "Giddap!"

Outcast struggled into a bumpy gallop, and many miles and many backward glances later, a jittery youth on a sweat-spattered horse arrived in Clinton and plunk in the midst of the Hell-Riders, a new Confederate cavalry regiment that had made the town its temporary headquarters. Streets and buildings swarmed with men in gray.

Seemingly everyone was an officer, and many of them captains and lieutenants but a year or two older than Wade. He would have gone galloping off, except that such obvious alarm in a stranger might be fatal.

He continued on quietly. With so many brave soldiers to glory in, no one appeared to notice a bedraggled civilian. He hitched Outcast in front of the Washington Hotel. Heart gonging, he worked his way through the crowd of soldiers to the clerk's desk.

The rooms were three dollars per day, and from a dollar up without meals. But there was no room at any price. The hotel was filled.

"You might try the Commercial on Bigler Street, my boy."

The volunteer of this intelligence, a courtly gentleman dressed entirely in black, had sidled to Wade's elbow. He hung there, disagreeably interested.

"Much obliged," mumbled Wade, and conscious of the man's scrutiny, pushed through the mass of sleek gray uniforms and into the street.

The Commercial Hotel, a ramshackle, two-story frame

structure, leaned at the edge of town. As Wade dismounted, he thought he glimpsed the man in black step furtively
into a dry goods shop across the street.

"You're jumpy as a bedspring," he rebuked himself.
Nevertheless, he had the pistol holsters slung in the crook
of his arm when he ventured into the lobby.

The place was a model of neglect, full of strong odors
and the gloom of slovenly old age. Four or five noncom-
missioned soldiers lounged in sagging chairs. Except for
glances of intolerant superiority — the kind a youth in
uniform bestows upon one who is not — they paid but
passing heed to Wade.

After providing for Outcast, Wade followed a large
Negro youth of his own age up one flight to a room above
the stables. Too tired to care about surroundings, Wade
stripped to the waist. Luke, the young slave, brought in
a bucket of water, a coarse towel, and the saddlebags and,
with a bow, departed.

Wade ducked his head in the bucket and the coldest
water in Virginia slopped over his wide shoulders. He
straightened, yelping. A vigorous towel-rub made do for
the rest of the dirt. Still shivering, he locked the door and
tucked the pistols beneath the pillow. Then he pulled the
grimy bed quilt to his chin and promptly sank into sub-
merging sleep. . . .

Gradually, insistently, the knocking registered through
the fathoms. He opened bleary eyes and blinked upon a
surface of darkness. "Who is it?"

"Luke, Marster Baxter. I fetched you some food."

Wade fumbled for a pistol. "W-what time is it?"

"Pas' dinner. You must be powerful hungry."

Wade lurched erect, rubbing the back of one hand across his mouth. He unlocked the door and squinted. Luke towered in the narrow hall.

"Come in," said Wade.

Luke entered, quick-stepping as though propelled from behind. The tray joggled in his hands, drawing Wade's gaze.

"Stand like that and do not move."

Wade froze obediently, arms at his sides and pistol pointed uselessly at the floor.

A Confederate colonel moved sternly from the doorway, his gun trained on Wade. Several white-haired civilians, including the man in black, strode in. Lamps were lighted, and the men commenced to ransack the room.

Wade was disarmed. The bedding was yanked apart, the saddlebags overturned and emptied. Aunt Mae's letters spilled out. The man in black knelt and rummaged through them.

"These seem to be all from an aunt, Colonel Mapes," he declared, disappointed.

Wade controlled a sigh of relief. Colonel Winslow's scheme of hiding the message to his brother among the packet of innocent personal papers seemed to have worked — till Colonel Mapes said:

"Better take them, Mr. Hinton. I shall want to inspect them myself later."

The officer dismissed Luke and considered Wade from head to toe. In his look was all the disdain of the high-born for the mobs of homespuns into whose society war had thrown him.

"These gentlemen are citizens of Clinton and members

of its Vigilance Committee," he told Wade. "They have requested that I conduct an inquiry into your presence in town. Every stranger falls under suspicion these days."

"I'm not a spy, if that's what you think."

"Then do you mind telling us, sir, why your horse bears a Union brand and carries regulation army equipment?"

The question, though asked in a polished tone, held embedded the knifelike conviction that Wade was a Federal soldier or agent. A hastily contrived denial would be cut to pieces.

Rather than be tripped in a lie, Wade related the events put in motion by the jinx. He omitted only the part concerning Colonel Winslow's message.

"I've been given two months' leave," he concluded. "You might call it a parole."

Colonel Mapes had heard the strange tale without interrupting. Now he asked politely if Wade didn't know that Abraham Lincoln had last week relieved General George McClellan of command of all the Union armies and placed him at the head of the Army of the Potomac.

"No," said Wade, shrugging.

"Southeastern Virginia," the colonel went on, "has become a field of primary action. McClellan undoubtedly will drive up the peninsula from Fort Monroe and attempt to take Richmond in April. Every man, every rifle will be needed, and *you* were allowed a vacation!"

"Nobody heard anything about General McClellan coming," objected Wade.

"Perhaps you have not heard there is a war, either," Colonel Mapes suggested sarcastically. "Have you questions, gentlemen?"

The committeemen had questions by the score. Wade replied lamely with "I don't know" or "I never heard that" to them all. He truthfully did not know one answer.

From questions about arms, supplies, and troops the emphasis shifted eventually to Wade Baxter, the typical Yank soldier. The stuffy chamber became a classroom, and Wade a pupil undergoing examination. Why had he enlisted? Was he opposed to slavery?

"I saw only three colored men before joining up," Wade faltered. "I never thought much about — "

He bit off the rest of the sentence in confusion. These sober, dedicated old Southerners unsettled him. They possessed a dignified nationalism which put to shame the rowdy blustering of the Federal camps. It was as if *their* cause were the right and righteous one.

He retreated into muteness and stubbornly let their questions roll off him. There came a point, however, when he hated his own confusion and ignorance more than he feared any punishment. Without regard to the consequences, he cried out:

"I enlisted to put down a rebellion, damn you!"

Colonel Mapes arched an eyebrow. "You are either a very stupid young man or an enormously daring actor." He laid an aristocratic hand on the chipped and battered door knob. "We have talked enough, gentlemen."

The Vigilance Committee filed out. The colonel, last to leave, removed the key from the inside of the lock.

"There is a guard posted outside this door, and another one on the street," he warned Wade. "Therefore I advise you to make yourself comfortable here."

"What are you going to do?"

"Have a close look at those letters," the colonel answered. "Then, if the committee decides you are not actively engaged in the war against the Confederate States of America, you will be sent to a prison camp."

"And if they decide differently?"

"Since you are wearing civilian clothes, you shall naturally be hanged as a spy."

The colonel shut the door. The key clanked in the lock. Wade was left in darkness.

He went immediately to the window. Presently the men who had been in the room appeared below. Colonel Mapes stopped and conferred briefly with four soldiers. Two took up positions where Wade could see them. The other pair scuttled out of sight.

"Gone round to the front," thought Wade, and wondered if Colonel Mapes had tempted him by asserting only one soldier, when actually four, guarded the street. If he were shot while trying to escape, how convenient! The old men of the Vigilance Committee might find comfort in the belief that only a guilty man attempts to flee. Moreover, they'd be spared the evil duty of a hanging.

Wade poked his head out the window and beheld a sheer two-story drop with nothing to clutch or break a fall. One of the soldiers lifted a carbine, motioning him back inside.

No chance of escape there. And no chance at all if he twiddled his thumbs while Colonel Mapes read through *all* the letters.

Wade examined the door. A beat-up, rickety panel of wood it was, but very definitely locked.

"Hey, Reb," he shouted.

"What is it, Yank?" answered a voice from the hall.

"I'm hungry. Can you get me something?"

"You jokin'? I can't leave this post."

"Let your partner stay."

"Ain't nobody here but me, Yank. The old man'd have me bucked and gagged iffen I prowled an inch."

"Aw, please," whimpered Wade.

"Go tuh hell," urged the Reb.

Wade grinned and picked up the saddlebags. The Reb was alone. That was precisely what he'd had to determine.

He gathered his belongings and packed them. Not a penny was missing from his clasp purse. The old men, however much they hated Yankee invaders, had declined to touch what was not rightfully theirs.

"Say, you up tuh somethin' in there, Yank?"

"I'm just chewing on the mattress," Wade called.

"You go ahead. Once you taste a Virginia mattress you won't ever eat Abe Lincoln's rations agin."

"It's mighty good, Reb. Mighty good," Wade agreed as he fitted the saddlebags and pillow over one shoulder, forming a cushion with which to ram the door.

"Don't try any tricks," the Reb warned suddenly. "I got me one of Colt's revolvin' rifles. Paid thirty dollars for it, all the money I had. And you know what? It can shoot for a week. So don't come bustin' through that door 'less you hanker to meet your Maker."

Wade shed the saddlebags and pillow as though they were the wings of doom. He visualized himself crashing blindly through the door, flying into the hall, and landing stunned and defenseless at the guard's feet.

He groped for another plan. If his mind lacked quickness in an emergency, it possessed the virtue of persistence. As he sat staring at the door, he seemed to wear two holes clean through.

What he saw in the hall was not a trained soldier, but a Southern boy who had spent all his money on a beautiful, shiny revolving rifle. As Wade saw this, the answer slipped into place.

The Reb must be coaxed into laying aside that rifle. More important, he must be persuaded to bring his head close to the door . . .

Wade replaced the saddlebags and pillow on his shoulder and slid ten dollars under the door. He left the bills protruding half on his side, where he could observe them.

"Hey, Reb!"

"What's it now, Yank?"

"You know what it is — food. You wouldn't object if I paid you for some, would you?"

Wade raised his voice slightly with each word as he retreated for a running start. The Reb must be deceived into thinking him still right at the door, too close to break it down.

The Reb snorted eloquently. "Greenbacks, ain't they?"

"And worth twice their value in Confederate currency," Wade reminded.

The opportunity to make a month's pay merely by stooping over produced a thoughtful silence. Temptation beckoned, and the proud but penniless owner of a new rifle submitted. Footsteps advanced cautiously, stopped, and then came the tap of a rifle being leaned against the wall.

"Just you scratch on the door some, so's I know where

you are," the guard directed. "I heard tell about pranks fellows can play with their voices."

Wade's hopes seesawed upon this unexpected demand.

"You're mighty scared of an unarmed man, Reb," Wade hurled mockingly. "A scared Reb like you wouldn't dare leave his post to buy a prisoner food. So maybe I'll just take back my money."

The Reb snarled his alarm and yanked.

As the bills vanished under the door, Wade catapulted through the air. One hundred and eighty pounds of mountaineer shattered the panel and went cannonballing into the stooping Reb.

Everything seemed crashing noise and splintering wood and tangled limbs. Wade powered the unconscious Reb along with him for several feet. The passageway trembled under the impact as they struck the floor together.

Wrenching free, Wade snatched the rifle and saddlebags and started for the main staircase.

"What's going on up there?" someone complained from the lobby.

Wade shrank from the top stair. A latch clicked behind him, a door squeaked. Hand on trigger, he spun and confronted Luke.

"This way," the young slave whispered. "Quickly!"

Footsteps mounted the stairs on the run.

Wade tightened his grip on the revolving rifle. With it he might hold the stairs against a company of men . . . for a while.

A soldier charged up the stairs. At the sight of Wade he uttered an astonished cry and fumbled for his pistol. He had it part way out when the butt of the revolving rifle sent him into a descending whirligig of arms and legs.

"Are there other stairs?" Wade snapped.

"This way," the slave repeated, and led Wade down a narrow back flight. They came to a landing, and the distant drone of voices carried through a small octagonal window.

Wade hissed for Luke to hold up. From the window he could view the street, and the group of men approaching.

Ten or twelve soldiers paraded in perfect step, as if to the beat of an invisible band. In front of them strode the men of the Vigilance Committee.

And in the lead marched Colonel Mapes. A pale downpour of moonlight washed him, glossing the rigid set of his jaw and whitening the backs of his long hands . . . hands which were expertly fashioning a rope into a hangman's noose.

## Chapter 3

# Bloodhounds

LUKE TUGGED WADE BY THE ARM. "COME," HE PLEADED IN a voice barely audible above the oncoming tramp of the lynchers.

Wade hung by the window. "Wait . . ."

A soldier had run over from across the street. He saluted Colonel Mapes and gestured at the second floor of the hotel.

"One of the two guards posted out front," Wade whispered. "That leaves one still unaccounted for."

The guard fell into stride by Colonel Mapes. A moment later their boots rang on the veranda steps.

Luke's tugging became frantic. The precious advantage of a head start was being squandered.

Wade quit the window and followed the slave down the remainder of the stairs and through a porter's anteroom. Luke signaled to a door, inched it open, and peered outside.

Above them the hotel awoke in a fury of slamming doors, rushing feet, and raging commands.

Luke darted into the alley and skimmed like a shadow along the wall. They had traveled the length of the hotel when Luke halted so abruptly that Wade bumped into his broad back.

Scarcely six feet distant and blocking their escape was the second guard.

Wade expected Luke to squash bone and outcry with a blow. But Luke twitched not a muscle. A lifetime of servitude prevented him from laying violent hands upon a white man.

Wade bounded around him, sacrificing silence for speed. The guard flung himself into position to meet the charge. Up flew his carbine; it misfired in a muffled click. He was desperately pumping the lever when Wade clubbed him.

Instantly Luke resumed the lead. They ran down every back alley in Virginia, or so it seemed to Wade, before Luke dodged into a stable.

"Are you home?" Luke panted, talking to darkness.

"Who comes?" inquired a voice.

"Friends of Uncle Abe," chanted Luke.

"What do you desire?"

"Light and loyalty."

Overhead a trap door squeaked and a rope ladder brushed Wade's arm as it uncurled to the floor. Luke nodded encouragement, and Wade climbed toward a square of total darkness.

Strong hands seized him and he let himself be hoisted into the attic, there to join an unwashed herd of the nation's hunted and oppressed. Four days and nights he lived in sunless, stinking squalor. He breathed air freshened only by the infrequent opening of the trap door as food was taken in and waste removed; or a frightened runaway accepted or relayed northward.

His refuge was the headquarters of the town's Loyal League, a society of Southern Negroes dedicated to the service of the Union. In the days Wade lay in hiding, he saw runaway slaves come and go, listened to the latest news of battle, and from Luke heard voiced the hope of a people adrift and divided.

"We do not all run," the dark-skinned boy said, tilting his head apologetically at a pathetic huddle of runaways. "Our young men are brave and wish to be soldiers for Abraham Lincoln."

"A good soldier is a careful one," Wade replied. "You should change your password each day."

Luke frowned. "It is what the Loyal League uses everywhere," he insisted stubbornly. "It would not be right to do different in Clinton."

Wade argued, but Luke refused to alter a ritual which to him symbolized a unity among his people, regardless of the danger. Nonetheless, that night he called up, "Are you home?" more cautiously than usual. He pulled himself through the trap and crawled to Wade. "We have a horse for you," he said. "Come."

Outside, the night smelled sweet after four days of being cooped in the attic. Wade filled his lungs greedily. By
the time he sat in the saddle his head had cleared, his
body felt limber again.

A feminine titter lilted nearby. Across the yard a pair
of lovers strolled arm in arm. They passed within a few
feet of the slave and the horseman. Wade did not draw
breath till the cooing and giggling had faded out of earshot.

Then he looked down at Luke, words of gratitude forming. He swallowed, and extended his hand.

Luke clasped it hesitantly. His upturned face held a
childlike eagerness and, somehow, a child's solemn longing.

"Do you think I'll make a soldier?"

"You'll make one helluva soldier," Wade said, and galloped out of Clinton.

His experience there had taught him several lessons in
surviving as a civilian. Foremost was that a hostile net-
work of home guardsmen — Vigilance Committees — existed throughout the Confederacy. If he were to reach his
Aunt Mae's cabin in Kentucky, towns and cities had to be
skirted.

What food he required he now purchased at small
farms, paying twenty or twenty-five cents for a once-a-day
meal of fried ham, sweet potatoes, and wheat cakes or bis-
cuits. He traveled slowly, both to conserve his horse and
to avoid attracting attention by undue haste. Three days
out from Clinton he forded the Roanoke River near the
North Carolina border.

It was then that he encountered the Negro-hunter.

At first he could not determine what had awakened him. He had bedded down beneath a star-encrusted sky, and suddenly he was blinking up into a pink haze of dawn-light. The small sounds of daybreak — the wind moving in the poplars, the earth creatures rousing — swam up to him, and with them floated the terrified moans of a human being.

Wade slipped the Navy Colt, which Luke had supplied, from the saddlebag beneath his head.

"Let go of that rope," he ordered.

The would-be horse thief dropped the picket rope as though it had stung him. His black, shaking hands lifted.

Eyeing Wade's gun, he began to sob and beg for his life.

The man was a runaway who was trying to get to the Loyal League at Clinton. More sense than that Wade could not make from his outpouring.

Suddenly the man's terror seemed to hop from his throat to his eyes, bulging them huge and white.

"You hear?" he moaned.

Wade heard . . . Far away dogs barked in the irregular rhythm of pursuit.

"Hounds," the slave whimpered.

Wade cocked his head, eerily enthralled. The runaway, left unminded, made a desperate lunge. He uprooted the picket iron and, raising it weapon-high, rushed recklessly for Wade.

The youth got the Colt around in time. The iron fell to the ground and sobs and begging poured out anew. Wade

felt anger and disgust. Yet if he didn't help him, the
wretch might lead the bloodhounds to the attic hideaway
of the Clinton Loyal League.

"Stay away from Clinton," he warned, heaving the saddle onto the horse's back. He buckled the cinch and fitted
the bridle. "Now go on."

The slave cowered, till he perceived Wade was in ear-
nest. Like a monkey he sprang into the saddle, and bab-
bling prayers disappeared beyond the crest of a hill.

The barking drew closer. To the south amber weeds
parted in twin lines as two dark reddish dogs came loping
up to the spot where the runaway had stood. They circled
and chased back and forth, sniffing and yipping in bewilderment. The deeply furrowed brows, drooping jowls, and
floppy ears gave them the look of two sad, puzzled old men.

Their antics engrossed Wade completely, and he was
unaware of the man till the third dog growled.

A low, vicious growl. It matched the dog — a gray brute
excessively proportioned in fang and jaw, the product of
breeding for fearlessness and schooling for hate. Such a
dog Wade had never before seen.

The man restrained the gray mongrel by a taut leash
while holding in his other hand a heavy musket. He called
sharply to the bloodhounds, and when they ambled to
him, hooked leashes to their collars and fed them from his
pocket. He squatted to inspect the ground, humming
pleasantly to himself. He poked a finger in the earth,
squinted northward in the direction of the hoofprints, and
finally acknowledged Wade's presence by a terse, "Your
horse?"

"Yes," replied Wade. "And if that was your slave who

stole him, you owe me three hundred dollars."

The man smiled, or, more accurately, did some mirthless sleight of lip that disclosed a jagged row of rotten teeth. He gave each dog a gentle pat and led them to Wade.

"Your horse cost me fifty dollars," he announced mildly. Yet his eyes were hard — harder than any Wade had ever looked into. All of the man had a lean, leathery, preserved hardness, as if long hours in the sun had baked the cruelty of his calling deep into his skin.

He gave Wade a handbill without comment. Wade read:

### No Tiss

The undersind makes it none that he is always redy to ketch runaways at best rates.

I have hed 15 years experience. My Runaway Hounds is the best in the State, and well trained.

My rates is 10 dollurs per hed if ketched in the beate where the Master lives, 15 dollurs in the cownty, and 50 dollurs out of the cownty.

Planters should take panes to let me know while the runaways tracks is fresh, if they want a good job.

Amos McCallahan.

"I come a pretty piece after them fifty dollars," McCallahan said.

The gray dog lifted from its loins, obeying some secret signal. McCallahan undid its leash, humming, as a housewife might set free a puppy to gambol on the lawn.

Wade got a hand inside his pocket, a finger around the trigger of the Colt. He would chance disrupting the countryside by shooting if need be, but he doubted his ability to shoot fast enough to beat both the mongrel's attack and McCallahan's musket.

"You don't have to lose your fifty dollars. I've got something to busy your dogs," said Wade.

He produced the Reb hat which had caught in the snare. "I'll pay twenty-five dollars now, and twenty-five when you find the owner."

McCallahan stroked the sweatband tentatively. "How long since he wore this?"

"Three, four days. You can pick up his trail about a mile down the road," Wade assured him.

The assurance was pure bluff. Wade knew that McCallahan wasn't fooled by any of his story. He let the bloodhounds smell the hat because he, too, stalled for time.

"The other twenty-five when you find him," Wade said emphatically.

McCallahan folded the bills. "You better come with me," he advised.

"I'll wait here."

The slave-hunter did not press the point. He fondled each dog, and the dread little procession moved downhill and out of sight in the valley below, the bloodhounds out in front and happily wagging their tails, the lean tracker next, and the gray dog trotting last.

It was a deadly game they played, the man and the youth. Both knew it. McCallahan would follow the bogus trail until he had figured a means of taking the rest of his fifty dollars. Wade had less than seven dollars left in his purse, and no choice but to flee.

He got just three yards. He pulled up, Indian-still, mistrusting his ears. From the valley resounded the last thing he ever expected to hear: the eager barking of dogs on a fresh scent.

Unbelieving, he tore down the side of a sloping field. He spied McCallahan bent over, removing the leashes from the bloodhounds' collars and fastening them to the shoulder harnesses, the position for tracking. With an impatient wrench, the team strained forward.

"*It can't be!*" Wade gasped.

He stepped onto the road, lured by the temptation of witnessing a duel between slave-hunter and Yankee-hunter. For once McCallahan's cruel skills would be well matched. He tracked a new kind of quarry, one possessing cunning, courage, and an unerring rifle.

Wade lagged several hundred yards behind the slave-hunter. In the burgeoning morning light, he dared not approach any nearer. He reached the point at which the dogs had picked up the trail, and looking back saw the high ground where he and McCallahan had met. Unquestionably, Three-Fingers had got this far, observed them, and retreated.

Ahead the bloodhounds lifted their noses continually to inhale the windborne scent. Wade had begun to fear Three-Fingers had taken to his spurs when the dogs veered off the road, and the chase continued through profusely wooded country.

Wade lost sight of McCallahan and had to guide himself by the barking. As he struggled along he wondered uneasily about Three-Fingers. His leaving the road for rough terrain made sense only if —

Two shots roared through the trees, as though meant

to confirm his suspicion. The barking lapsed into strangled, short-lived yelps of pain. Wade heard McCallahan's oath of surprise and the threshing of a body seeking cover. Then a heavy silence collected above the ambush.

The next sound was a vicious, deep-throated snarl. The gray dog, Wade thought; the gray dog doing what it had been blooded and trained to do. He hearkened for the screams of a man being ripped by those lancelike fangs. Instead, there came a third report, and immediately afterward the answering boom of a musket. McCallahan had sacrificed the mongrel for one clear shot.

The shooting ceased, and there was an inflow of unnatural stillness, as when all sound subsides, but not all movement. Wade crept forward. After some moments, a horse whinnied nervously, and a man soothed it, whispering. A creak of saddle leather under a load, an urging tongue-cluck, and the survivor of the contest rode off unseen.

Wade slipped cautiously between the intervening trees and looked around at those who would never depart.

Of the bullets exchanged, three had killed the dogs. The fourth and last one fired — the one from McCallahan's musket — had missed. For if it had wounded Three-Fingers, he could not have used the saber so murderously.

The blade had been thrust into the slave-hunter's throat. Wade shivered in horror at McCallahan's end. With what appalling ease he had been overcome!

The man who accomplished this was still at large. Most likely, Wade reasoned, he had ridden back to the road. Hence the youth, in resuming his westward journey, shied from the thoroughfares and exploited every foot of woods and ravines.

By noon he had come to a large pasture. He started across it, intent upon a handsome stallion romping with two mares and their foals. Halfway across he heard a blood-curdling Rebel yell. A troop of cavalry had swung from course and was bearing down upon him.

Wade attempted to cut back. One column of horsemen drove between him and the trees. The other column flanked wide in a circling movement.

Wade drew his Colt — and had it shot spinning from his grip.

"You led us a merry chase, Baxter," Colonel Mapes said, reining up, a smoking pistol in his hand.

Wade planted himself and glared defiantly at the colonel and his soldiers. He saw youths attired in fine uniforms whose newness the dust of the trip could not disguise. To them the long ride had been a challenging adventure in horsemanship; to them the hanging of a Yankee was an extra fillip in the bright new game of war.

Colonel Mapes sat his horse like an emperor, unrestrained by a council of elders. The white-haired men of the Clinton Vigilance Committee were miles away. Here he ruled with the authority of life and death.

"Tie his hands behind his back."

Wade downed the first three who tried. A swarm of reinforcements smothered him, rolled and trussed him. He was hauled, kicking and struggling, toward the trees.

Rough hands wrestled him upon a horse. A rope was draped around a branch above his head, and other hands fought to seize the descending noose and fit it about his neck. A squabble developed as to who should have the honor. In those lost seconds, Wade's life was spared.

For a bearded Reb major came galloping madly up to the tree, thundering curses. By the look of him he had no part in Colonel Mapes' shiny new outfit. Bareheaded and dirt-spattered, he rode a worn-out horse like a no-nonsense veteran and raked the astonished youngsters with a coldly furious eye and fiery tongue.

"Which of you idiots is Mapes?" he bellowed. When informed, he commenced to berate the higher-ranking officer as though he were the rawest of recruits.

What was he doing chasing a single Yank with half his regiment? Why wasn't he moving to Yorktown? What, he hadn't received orders! Damn! Didn't he know the Yankees were building up at Fort Monroe? Harvey Hill wanted every available regiment —

Colonel Mapes broke in hotly, demanding the major's credentials. He read them, paling, while the soldiers and officers made sheepishly for their stirrups.

In the commotion, the major had maneuvered beside Wade.

"When I shoot, fall as if you're hit."

The major went skittering off, cursing with renewed vigor, and Wade wasn't sure he'd heard correctly.

Colonel Mapes returned the papers. "Wilson and Morgan — finish Baxter."

"Don't waste any *more* time!" shouted the major. He drew his pistol and fired twice.

Wade slid off the horse untouched. Curled on his side, he heard the trample of hoofs, the major shouting, "Get back to Clinton and march your men, colonel! I'll bury him."

The earth trembled as fifty horses dug into a gallop. The hoofbeats had diminished to a faint drumming when the major ran over and, shoving and pushing, got Wade up behind the saddle.

"My hands," gasped Wade.

"No time. Cling with your knees, lad."

Dazedly, Wade did as he was bade, and the pair went at a punishing clip for three or four miles. Once the major inquired if Wade could hold on a little longer. And once he snapped, "I'll explain later." He did not speak again till he had dismounted.

He hustled Wade to a slatted barn of the kind used in curing tobacco. He placed one hand against the door, and panted, "Hurry, before we are seen!"

Wade backed off, jerking crazily at his bonds.

For the hand which the major had placed against the door was his left hand. And it had but three fingers.

*Chapter 4*

# Hobnob in a Hogshead

THE MAJOR GRINNED MALICIOUSLY AS HE THRUST WADE inside. "I couldn't let them hang you after I've gone to so much trouble."

He tipped over one of the large wood casks that cluttered the barn and settled himself on it comfortably.

"If they hanged you, there'd be all those witnesses to the deed," he resumed. "Mapes' regiment will probably be locking with your Fifty-sixth on the peninsula before long, and one of those witnesses might be captured. It wouldn't do for anyone, even a Confederate prisoner, to see a hanged man walking around full of life!"

Three-Fingers paused briefly to enjoy Wade's puzzlement.

"In my plan, the Wade Baxter who returns to his regiment can tell a tale of harrowing escape — with no witnesses to stumble onto the lie. What is the lie? Let me see
. . . The two shots I fired at you missed. You played dead,
and when I went to bury you, you leaped up, overpowered
me, and rode off on my horse. The Sergeant Baxter who
tells that yarn, my boy, will be the lion of the Union
camps."

Wade gritted his teeth and yanked futilely at the ropes
around his wrists. He couldn't follow the Reb, especially
the odd way he referred to *the* Sergeant Baxter.

"If you don't intend to kill me, untie my hands," he
demanded.

"Oh, I don't mean quite that," Three-Fingers corrected,
smirking. "Unless you are dead you can't come to life."

"I'm no good at riddles."

"Try something easier. When is a double trouble?"

Three-Fingers held out a tintype, which Wade remembered having had taken of himself the first day in uniform.

"I sent that picture to my Aunt Mae — !"

"And she gave it to me. Rather, she showed it to me,
and liking it so very much, I kept it."

"If you harmed her!"

"Your sweet, gentle Aunt Mae? Certainly not. I was
peddling notions — Buttons! Ribbons! Needles! — and she
purchased two dollars' worth. We had a nice chat, and
she brought out your letters and said how proud she was
of her boy in blue."

Three-Fingers replaced the tintype in his blouse. "You
write an excellent letter for a Yank, full of charming de-

tails. But I'm getting ahead of myself. I should explain what I was doing in Kentucky.

"I was sent there to assist the Copperheads in bringing the state into the Confederacy." Three-Fingers shrugged moodily. "Alas, Kentucky is going to stay with the Union. So I started back to Richmond, posing as a peddler. When your picture and letters fell into my hands, the failure of my mission seemed trivial. I possessed the means of striking a harder blow for freedom than anyone had dreamed."

He scrutinized Wade. "You still don't understand? All right, I'll put it differently. Your letters home provide a priceless account of your every experience in the army, what you've done, what you expect to do. A man wishing to impersonate you could have no better record to study — "

"A man wishing to impersonate me," broke in Wade, "has to resemble me."

"I know of one who is your double," said Three-Fingers. "Captain Roger Bragg of General Joseph E. Johnson's command. A year or two older than you, perhaps, and not quite so tall. But a good enough likeness to pass muster."

"You've gone to a lot of trouble," said Wade, "over a common soldier."

"The new Sergeant Baxter will not be a common soldier. He was trained at the Point. Within a month he'll be a dispatch rider. Oh, he'll perform his duties nobly in skirmishes. Then one afternoon, when a hundred thousand men are closed in battle, a message will never get delivered. A Union corps will not advance, a Union battery will not open fire, a division of reserves will wait and wait to move into line. Wars turn on less, Baxter."

Three-Fingers left the cask. His eyes glittered like a fox's. "I show you a second tintype."

Wade stared. The portrait Three-Fingers showed him might have been of himself, except for the West Point cadet's uniform.

"Two years ago I didn't have this beard," explained Three-Fingers. "Bearded, I am Roger Bragg. Clean shaven, I shall become Wade Baxter. I will return to the Fifty-sixth as you and will immediately ask for a transfer to a headquarters company. With the stigma of a jinx still about, your old colonel will be glad enough to be rid of 'Sergeant Wade Baxter.' "

"You'll give yourself away in two days," blurted Wade. "Somebody will notice the missing finger."

"Are you trying to convince *me* of that — or *yourself?*" Roger Bragg chuckled. "Now, once again! When is a double trouble? No? The answer, of course, is when both doubles are alive. To eliminate that inconvenience — "

"Come out with your hands up — both of you!"

Roger Bragg had raised his gun barrel to Wade's forehead. He stiffened, but did not alter his pose.

"Pull the trigger, major, and you'll end up in a muddy ditch with the flies on you."

The voice was cheerfully firm. Bragg released the gun.

An iron-gray, thickset old man leaned upon a crutch, pistol in hand. He seemed almost jolly at first glance, and hardly up to ordering Roger Bragg about for long. Yet his queer bright eyes and the swiftness with which he perceived Wade's bonds suggested something other than a typical small planter.

"This is my barn, my land, and Otto Decker is my name," he said. "You have names, gentlemen?"

"Roger Bragg. Major, Confederate States of America. He is a spy."

"I'm not," retorted Wade. "My name is Wade Baxter. I'm on my way to Kentucky."

"The boy lies," Bragg asserted blandly. He lowered his hands, as though the victim of a silly oversight.

Decker made a menacing sound. "Hold them high, please, major," he requested. "That's it."

In that momentary flare of anger Wade got an inkling of tremendous evil about the old man, though only an inkling.

Decker relieved Bragg of his sidearm. "We have a regular puzzle here, don't we, major? I'm a great one for puzzles and riddles. When is a double trouble, you asked?"

"If you are a loyal Southerner, Mr. Decker, you will forget what you overheard," Bragg warned.

Decker puckered his brow. "I was born plumb in the middle of New Hampshire. Does that make me a Southern Yank or a Northern Reb? Dear me, but there's a riddle for *you*, major."

"Mr. Decker —— "

"As to loyalty, major, I see mighty little profit in that. I grow tobacco — or did. My seed beds are down, but who's to transplant? My hands all run north."

"Well, at least you are an honest man, and I admire that," commended Bragg. He smiled disarmingly. "I am sure you will want to be fair. All right, then. I shall leave this prisoner with you. I am needed in Richmond."

The innocent offer, Wade knew, would bring the queer old man to his death by nightfall.

Decker wasn't taken in. He cocked an eyebrow and scratched among the roots of his beard. "I want to be fair," he agreed, a slyness in his tone. "Fair to *both* of you." He untied Wade's wrists and signaled Roger Bragg to lower his hands. "Come along, gentlemen."

Managing crutch and gun cleverly, he escorted them into the house. In the hot, musty parlor he took two shiny pistols from a bureau drawer and stuck them into his belt, pirate style.

"Otto?"

Wade turned quickly to a red velvet chair by the window. He saw a tiny old woman, a withered remnant of calico and papery flesh. Lusterless eyes lit slowly in alarm.

Decker bent over her and tenderly kissed the parched forehead. "We have visitors, sweetheart."

"Not the hogsheads!" she whimpered. "They're both so young, Otto!"

"The major tells riddles. Think of it!"

The woman tried feebly to object, twisting and curling in the chair like a scorched leaf. Decker touched her shoulder and motioned Wade and Bragg outside.

"My wife is not a lover of riddles," he apologized. "To the barn, gentlemen."

Bragg scowled. "What kind of joke is this, sir?"

"A riddle, Major Bragg. You will especially enjoy it, being partial to riddles."

The old man marched them to the barn and down along the rows of hogsheads. Coming to three oversized casks set in an equilateral triangle, he gave the command to halt.

"These three hogsheads were built by my wife's great-grandfather," he said. "You will notice they are much larger than the others — four feet across and more than eight feet high. They have a curious history."

He patted one of the casks affectionately. "In the early days the charges for handling tobacco were so much per hogshead, rather than so much per pound. Naturally, planters made their hogsheads bigger and bigger so as to hold more and more tobacco. These three were the biggest ever built in Virginia. Unfortunately, they were so enormous they defeated their purpose. No one would handle them. So for a century they stood idle. Trouble was, everybody saw them simply as tobacco casks."

The old man banged his crutch on the floor twice, an action like a cackle of glee.

"I saw them as something else," he said. "As a means to a unique contest of wits. Oh, you will find that out, dear me, yes!"

He tossed a pistol to Wade and one to Bragg. "They are quite empty, gentlemen. I shall insert two bullets into each hogshead."

Through narrow slots cut in the casks about five feet from the bottom Decker distributed the ration of bullets. He bustled from cask to cask in the high spirits of a man about to unveil a wonder of his ingenuity.

"The rules are simple," he said. "Each of you will climb into a hogshead. Through the slot you will be able to see the other two hogsheads. You have only to reason out which hogshead holds your opponent. You have a pistol, and once inside the hogshead, two bullets. Fire at the wrong hogshead and you give yours away. Any questions?"

Bragg said, "What if we refuse to play your game?"

"Oh, no one refuses to play *hobnob in a hogshead!*" the old man exclaimed indignantly, and brandished his pistol.

Bragg's cheeks whitened with rage. "Let's get on with it," he said scornfully.

"Good." Decker thumped his crutch. "We begin. First, please lean against this hogshead."

The prisoners leaned as directed, hands overhead and laid upon the hogshead, feet well out in the rear. To attempt a sudden move from this awkward position was impossible. The old man put blindfolds on them and walked them to the center of the triangle.

"I shall turn you around twenty times," he announced. "After that, I shall lead you each to a hogshead. When I cry climb, you are to pull yourself to the top. Do not drop inside till I shout drop. That way, neither of you will be able to get inside and pull off the blindfold before the other."

The old man rotated Wade round and round. The youth could only guess the same indignity was befalling Roger Bragg. When the count reached twenty, the old man steered him tottering to a hogshead and guided his right hand to the top edge.

A minute later came the command, "Climb!"

Wade scrambled up the side of the hogshead and sat straddling the rim. He hadn't a clue to Bragg's whereabouts. To cover the noise of the climbing, the old man had pounded his crutch against the staves of a cask, creating a confusion of great echoing booms.

Then, like the hushing of ceremonial drums, the booms

ceased. Wade tensed, awaiting the next command.

"Drop!"

Wade kicked his outside leg over and slid down inside the hogshead. His left foot struck bottom first; his left knee buckled, flopping him on his ribs. He tore off the blindfold and discovered almost total darkness in the cask's depths. He felt about for the two bullets and listened for Bragg.

"You're a pair of beauties," Decker crowed. "Dear me, you're a treat to watch! One as agile as the other. Now that you're tucked in cozy, I leave you to discover which has the quicker wits."

His footsteps held the trace of a swagger as they made toward the door. Before they faded completely, Wade had the two bullets. He inserted them into the chambers of the pistol and peered through the eye slot.

The other two hogsheads in the triangle were visible in the dim light. But the eye slots were blended over and lost in the shadows. Wade's hope of spotting Bragg behind his narrow window went aglimmering.

There was one consolation: Bragg peered out upon the identical sight. And one anxiety: Bragg had all the advantage in cunning.

This knowledge hounded Wade. He tried to dislodge it from his mind. "You've a gun and two bullets, and he's got the same," he encouraged himself. "Now *think*."

He thought of two courses of action.

*He could fire one bullet into each hogshead.* By aiming where he judged the eye slot to be, he would kill Bragg — provided that the Reb was peering out and not curled on the floor. If he did not kill Bragg, the results were disastrous: he was left with an empty pistol, while Bragg had two bullets and knew where to fire them.

*He could fire both bullets into one hogshead.* By aiming one high and one low, his chances of at least wounding the Reb were excellent. Then if he instantly jumped out of the hogshead while Bragg was still stunned, he might make good an escape. The obvious flaw: into *which* hogshead was he to fire both bullets?

He was back where he started.

The two hogsheads bulked flatly alike. "About as alike as a sack of flour and a sack of gunpowder," thought Wade.

Inside the barn there was not a rustle of clothing or a creak of boots. Wade's own breathing dinned in his ears.

Bragg was waiting. Unquestionably, the Reb had rejected any ideas calling for him to commit himself. He was content to let Wade declare.

So with neither willing to shoot first, the contest evolved into a stalemate, into the test of patience and raw nerve. Or did it? Suppose they refused to shoot one another? Suppose they joined against the common enemy, Otto Decker?

Wade had put his mouth near the eye slot when he realized what he was doing. Bragg would draw a bead on him with the first whispered syllable. The Reb had surely considered such an alliance, and the fatal consequences to whoever voiced the offer.

Wade hunkered down on his heels weakly. Bragg would always be a thought ahead. All right, recognize the fact. Concede the Reb the ability to solve the riddle in time. What could be done?

One thing. Force him to act before he was ready.

Although this course meant revealing his own position, Wade decided to gamble. Once each knew where the other was, intellect counted for little. The contest would come down to a trial of courage. And in that department Wade conceded nothing.

He chose the right-hand hogshead for the first bullet. At best, it would kill Roger Bragg outright. At worst, it would pierce an empty hogshead, and Bragg's return shot would slay him. With any kind of luck, however, he would get off with but a flesh wound on the first round of fire.

He devoted several minutes to the best defense against the Reb's bullet. He pondered a dozen positions, settling finally upon a semi-crouch to the left of the eye slot. He wiped perspiration from his face and squinted into the barn. He aimed the pistol.

His finger was hard on the trigger when something plopped on the roof. A bird alighting. Wade looked up instinctively, and glimpsed the one position he'd overlooked. *Up.*

"Bragg might fire high or low into the hogshead, right or left, but he won't fire above the level of my head," Wade thought. In the top two feet of the eight-foot hogshead lay perfect safety!

Wade doffed his boots and began working his way to the top of the cask. Back pressed against one wall and stockinged feet braced against the opposite, he toiled like an Alpinist hunching up a narrow rock chasm. At the top, he shifted into a more compact position.

His left side faced the bottom, permitting him to look down into the blackness. With the look his confidence faltered. He could no longer distinguish the eye slot. Having lost that, he lost his sense of direction and all concept of where the other two hogsheads were placed.

Part of his plan — the shot to draw the Reb's fire — might still be put into effect. But a shot fired at random would not fulfill his original hope of dealing a wound.

"I might just as well holler where I am and save a bullet," Wade thought despairingly.

A second later there wasn't any need to shoot or to shout.

A gun exploded from the right and wood splintered below him. Bragg had declared!

It came to Wade suddenly. *Of course!* The Reb had reached the same conclusion about the height of the hogshead — but a minute sooner. Both were now curled at the top, and though Bragg had guessed correctly between the two hogsheads confronting him, he had wasted one of his bullets!

"Go and figure out why I didn't fire back," Wade taunted under his breath.

The Reb was an unmissable target. If Wade shot toward the source of the gunfire, at a level equal to himself, he must wound or kill.

As he was jubilantly musing upon the change in fortunes he heard Bragg climb out of his hogshead.

The Reb's reasoning was clear. Since Wade did not fire back immediately, then he must be lying dead or mortally wounded.

The footsteps stopped. The Reb was testing his theory, exposing part of himself — enough of a part for Wade to see through the eye slot, if he could see.

The footsteps started again. In long, light bounds they

reached Wade's hogshead. Wade cocked his pistol.

He heard a grunt of annoyance — the impenetrable darkness of the hogsheads had thwarted the Reb's attempt to see into the eye slot. For a timeless moment nothing occurred. Then the great cask groaned, swayed, and a three-fingered hand coiled talonlike over the rim. Its strong and perfect mate appeared beside it, gripping the pistol. Clothing brushed softly up and up, buttons rattling against wood. . . .

Then all at once a face was rising between the hands.

The pistols roared together. Only Wade's scored its mark. Explosions of flame and choking acrid smoke shrouded the face. Wade squeezed the trigger wildly, and then again and again, the hammer striking upon empty chambers. The hands retracted; Bragg crashed backward to the floor.

Trembling, Wade climbed out of the cask. In the stillness of the late afternoon, time and reality surged back to him. He heard far off the dragging steps and punctuating thump of Otto Decker.

"Now to put an end to your murdering pastime," thought Wade grimly.

He scaled the third hogshead, seeking the two bullets cast there at the start. His fingertips found something — a pebble.

Wade dropped the empty pistol, squatted and spread both hands. His palms grazed a surface bumpy with hard, bullet-shaped objects, and a cold horror replaced his soaring confidence.

For he understood then the enormity of Otto Decker's twisted mind. Without bringing the objects to his eye, he knew they were pebbles, every one of them, and that pebbles were all the crafty old man put into the third cask.

Wade shuddered. Each pair of pebbles meant one round and one victim of hobnob in a hogshead; and the pebbles lay upon the bottom of the third cask as thick as moss upon a forgotten grave.

## Chapter 5

# Belle Isle

WADE GATHERED A FISTFUL OF PEBBLES AS OTTO DECKER rapped his pistol against the hogshead, summoning him to climb out and claim his reward.

Wade straightened slowly. He pictured the reward in store for him. The fact that Decker continued to be amused by hobnob in a hogshead spoke with crimson eloquence. No one — winner or loser — was ever allowed to bear tales.

"I bet on the other fellow," Decker confessed as Wade emerged. "He had a cleverness about him. I never reckoned a slow-moving youngster like you could solve it."

"I didn't," said Wade curtly. His right hand tightened over the pebbles, a blinding dose for the old man's eyes. But he didn't fling them. The perfect opportunity never quite came. An hour later, the pebbles grated heavily in his pocket as he tossed down the shovel. "Now what?"

Otto Decker hobbled over and inspected the two graves which Wade had dug. "Now carry out Major Bragg."

Wade tensed, knowing for whom the second grave was intended.

The pistol jumped to life in Decker's hand. "Carry him out!" he snarled.

Anger and fright swelled like a huge lump in Wade's throat, but he obeyed. He preceded Decker through the barn, as the thumps of the crutch accented the terrible silence that overlaid the rows of hogsheads.

Suddenly the silence was wracked by a clash of noises — Decker's shrill cry of alarm, a metallic clatter, and a swift padding of feet.

Spinning, Wade saw Decker stagger backward, clutching his wrist, whimpering, and fumbling for his crutch. A tall black figure was picking up the pistol from the floor.

"Luke!"

Luke did not answer. He seemed absolutely terrified by what he had done. Trembling, he watched the white man rub his wrist where it had been struck.

"Luke!" repeated Wade. "It's all right. He was going to kill me."

The young slave recovered himself with a shiver. Wordlessly he delivered the gun into Wade's keeping.

Otto Decker began to whine obsequiously. In the moment since his tumble from captor to captive, he had become a scared and helpless old invalid. With exaggerated smiles and imploring hands he begged Wade to believe that he never purposed him harm.

Wade was moved to pity. He relaxed his grip on the pistol till he realized Decker had slyly inched to where a swing of the crutch would brain him.

"Get back!" Wade warned. Decker retreated, muttering wrathfully, and eyed the two boys like a lame and hungry old lion.

Wade shifted his attention to Luke. "How did you find me?" he asked in amazement.

The feat sounded simple — from Luke's lips. A Rebel major had ridden into Clinton soon after Wade had ridden out. The major had inquired after a youth whose dress and description matched Wade's, and, after speaking with the clerk at the Commercial Hotel, the officer was not long in getting onto the road Wade had taken. Luke had stolen a horse and followed.

"When I saw you diggin' the two graves," the young slave said calmly, "I sneaked into the barn and hid behind the casks."

Before Wade could express his gratitude or explain about the major, Otto Decker gave a laugh.

The creak of carriage wheels sounded outside.

Wade rushed to the side of the barn. Through the slats he spied a horse and buggy stopping. A man carrying a black bag alighted and entered the farmhouse.

Evidently the man was a doctor. Wade saw him bend solicitously over Decker's wife, and then immediately disappear from the window. "He's coming out!"

"Doc Moser is a captain in the irregulars around here," said Decker. "When he sees what you and this slave did to a Confederate officer he won't be very happy."

"Can your horse carry two?" Wade shot at Luke.

"For a piece."

"We've got to hurry."

The two youths sprinted from the barn. Wade seized the reins and, with Luke up behind, goaded the horse into a gallop.

For perhaps a mile they rode at full speed. The farm had passed beyond sight when Wade slowed the tiring animal to a walk and told Luke about Roger Bragg and the deadly game they had played in Decker's barn.

"The doctor will have soldiers out hunting us," Wade declared. "You'd better go back to Clinton. I can hide out somewhere till night."

Luke's voice was strangely low as he replied, "I can't go back to Clinton, Marster Baxter. I stole a horse, and I hit a white man's wrist."

Wade flushed. For sixteen years he had lived in America in freedom: for sixteen years Luke had lived as a slave in the same country. Yet courage had lifted them both to the same level.

"We'll go on together," Wade said.

Behind him he thought Luke breathed a pleased sigh.

So they rode as Wade and Luke, and the word "marster" was not used. They were friends.

In choosing a course west, Wade held to the natural depressions of the land. He was aware that any pursuers, using the roads, might gain upon them rapidly. Yet he himself could not use the roads and risk the singular spectacle of white and black astride one horse.

They arrived at a plantation when Luke said, "The Sumner place. Stop. My aunt is cook there. She'll feed us good, and she'll know where the stallions is hid."

In the concealment of a bordering wood the boys waited for night. Then Luke started across the fields toward the slave cabins.

Almost as soon as Luke blended into the darkness, Wade heard the soldiers. Five men galloped up, sitting their saddles lightly, prepared to rise in the stirrups like searchers. The leader raised his hand, and the horsemen gathered in a circle a hundred feet from Wade. The leader gestured toward the big, colonnaded plantation house and toward the wood. He decided on the wood.

They approached silently, spread out in a miniature battle line, carbines unslung and ready. Wade retreated, but couldn't escape. The wood was too shallow, the trees too sparsely spaced. He would have to pick off two or three, and with luck discourage the rest.

Aiming at the nearest rider, he thought, "The doctor ought to have sent more than five."

There were more — seven more — and they came at him from the rear. Wade never saw the rifle stock that drove him to the ground. A booted foot kicked the pistol from his fingers. A voice above him asked, "What about the slave?"

"Probably gone after food," came the answer. "Sergeant Van Bryn, take two men and search the slave quarters. The boy's about sixteen. He was wearing a hotel porter's white shirt and trousers. Get him any way you have to."

Wade's head throbbed as though it would split. His dulled senses registered voices and motions indistinctly. He was thrown upon a horse, but not given the reins. A long ride, a command to dismount — and a candle was thrust hotly to his face. Otto Decker's voice asserted, "He's the one, doctor."

A discussion ensued in which Decker's request to punish Wade was refused. A new batch of guards, apparently regulars, took charge of Wade. More riding after that. Finally a soldier said, "All right, Baxter. Get down."

His elbow was taken and he was jostled toward a brick building.

"What's the kid done? Raided a nursery?"

"Shot and wounded one of our officers," was the unjoking retort.

*Wounded.* The word sliced through the fuzzy ache in Wade's head. Had he heard correctly? "How badly is the major hurt?" he gasped.

"How should I know, Yank," the soldier at his arm said. As though glad his night's chore was ended, he pushed Wade into a wide room containing several score of Northern prisoners.

Before long two armed Rebels entered and began to "trade" with him. In return for his fine store clothes, he acquired a homespun shirt, a pair of filthy britches, and shoes which fitted perfectly once he'd cut holes for his toes. He managed to slip the little money he possessed under an armpit.

In the morning the captives were paraded outside and, under a sky of leaden clouds, formed into a column of pairs. Eastward they marched, toward Richmond and the notorious island prison, Belle Isle.

They trudged in benumbed despair, seldom glancing at the guards. The hopelessness of their plight united them in clannish misery. They were without the joy of victory, without the honor of valiant defeat. They were soldiers who had failed. They moved like sleepwalkers. Wade, having been unable to learn anything of Major Roger Bragg, soon fell under the spell of abject gloom.

After toiling fifteen miles or so, the ragged column had a respite near a village. Soon an aged Negro peddler appeared, lugging kettles of buckwheat batter and corn batter. He baked cakes, three for five cents, on order for the Southerners. When he tried to sell some to the prisoners he was chased off, though not before uttering one sentence.

"Luke, he say he follow," the old man whispered to Wade.

Luke was safe and had evaded capture! Wade felt a thrill of hope, and vented his excitement in building the wildest air castles. He saw himself escaping and rewarding the noble and loyal Luke by buying his freedom.

A muzzle prodded his ribs. The order to resume marching was shouted. The dreams vanished in the dust of the road. Common sense reasserted itself, and he began to pray that Luke did not attempt some foolhardy act against the stoutly manned column.

Luke attempted nothing more rash than to assure Wade he was not forsaken. Twice he allowed Wade a glimpse of him — once sitting with a wooden fishing pole by a roadside creek, once ambling innocently in the distance. And on the last day of the grueling march, Wade saw his friend standing helplessly on a Richmond street corner as the column crossed to Belle Isle.

The aspect of the island, as Wade set foot upon it,

seemed to belie the stories he had heard on the march. The main part was covered with trees and sward, and despite the scattered pieces of artillery, he encountered nothing which violated the code of war and human decency.

Then he had reached a bluff, and he could look down upon the stockade.

The prisoners were there, on a sandy, open rectangle of about four acres, slightly elevated above the bordering James River. Enclosing the stockade was an earthwork three feet in height, with deep ditches running on both sides. All around the edge of the outer ditch were the guards, about forty feet apart. Large, bell-shaped Sibley tents, pitched in regular rows, spread over a small portion of the shadeless pen. Still, except for the unbelievable crowding, the area looked to Wade very much like an ordinary encampment.

The resemblance lasted until he was ordered down into the stockade.

There men like skeletons risen from the tomb, foul-smelling and half naked, tottered forward. "Fresh fish! Fresh fish!" The cry announced the new arrivals to all parts of the area.

A few heads poked out of the tents inquisitively. They pulled back, their owners snarling at the opportunists who, hopeful of snatching their places under the shelter, crept near like jackals.

When it was found that the newcomers hailed from Kentucky, Michigan, and New York, separate groups attached to each. About twenty Kentuckians beset Wade.

They peppered him with questions, none of which he

could answer. The men, their families, their home towns, were strange to him. Neither did he know of the recent battles — what had happened at Centreville, Leesburg, Newbern, Acquira Creek. Rumors had an exchange officer conferring with Major Turner, the prison commander. Was it true?

Five or six times the questions were repeated. Finally Wade spread his hands and walked away. Several of the more determined prisoners nagged at his heels, assuring him there was to be an exchange with the Rebs. Why hadn't he heard? Their anger was pathetic.

He found a patch of clean, dry sand and sat down. Eventually the last of his circle slunk away, berating him and bolstering each other with assurances of an exchange.

Wade closed his eyes. He had never experienced nausea, but for the next little while the island spun away from him in a yellow fog. The grueling march had drained him physically; and now, the overpowering stench and the spectacle of thousands of human scarecrows herded together in misery churned his insides.

When he returned to himself again, he began to wander about the enclosure, his stomach trembling.

Across the James River he could behold Richmond. The capital of the Confederacy stretched tauntingly near, barely half a mile to the east. Yet so unlike Belle Isle was it in the privileged lives of its dwellers that it appeared, with the afternoon sun slanting off its spires and roofs, like a jeweled city on a faraway planet.

"It can be reached," he thought, estimating the width of the river. "At night . . . before I'm too weak . . ."

Just then a pair of hands seized him and yanked violent-
ly. Wade sailed backward. He wrenched loose, cursing,
prepared for anything.

A gaunt, gangling prisoner with a lantern jaw grinned at
him. "You're solid as a bull, brother. You must be new —— "

"What the dickens was the idea of *that!*" demanded
Wade, straightening his shirt.

The gaunt man pointed a brown finger at the inner
ditch and at the guards stationed on the planks of the
earthwork. "Those people don't like Yanks much. They
shoot when one of us gets within three feet of that ditch.
It's called the deadline for a mighty good reason."

Wade said sheepishly, "S-sorry, I didn't —— "

The gaunt man cut the apology with a friendly wave.
"I used to be a deacon," he said. "I sort of got into the
habit of trying to save lives. If you'll come with me, I'll
show you around this resort."

For the rest of the afternoon, Wade tagged after his pro-
tector, learning the routine of the island. He had one burning question; he refrained from asking it till the evening
rations were distributed.

"Corn bread and soup twice a day," the gaunt man said,
gobbling hungrily. "Meat three times a week. On the meat
days, less bread."

The gaunt man's ability to devour such food with gusto
astonished Wade, who merely sniffed his portion. Around
him the other prisoners ate noisily as hogs. In a fit of
furious impatience, he hurled out the question. "Haven't
you thought of escaping?"

The gaunt man spat out a chunk of cob as though he

hadn't heard. "Eat," he said. "Or you'll wake up tonight chewing on your sleeve."

"Escape!" Wade hissed. *"Escape!"*

The gaunt man continued to eat, pushing his large jaw, munching the last of the corn bread. He licked his lips; then he dabbed his fingers around the corners of his mouth and licked his fingertips.

He said, "There are two routes a man might take if he yearned after the blessings of hardtack and coffee — and if he wasn't all used up by the winter frost or the summer sun."

Wade shifted so that the gaunt man need not raise his voice.

"There's the river," the gaunt man said. "And there's the two bridges from the mainland to the iron works on the high ground. Either way, a man's got the same problems — the guards and those pieces of artillery."

"You can't have given up!" Wade exclaimed. "I don't believe you've stopped thinking about getting out!"

"Everybody thinks about that," said the gaunt man softly. "Now come along, or there won't be any beds left."

The sun had declined to a tip-top arc of orange-red at the horizon, and a chilling river wind swept across the barren four acres. The prisoners were bedding down in long rows under the open sky. The gaunt man knelt at the end of a row and began to scoop sand with both hands. He made depressions for his hips and shoulders.

"We sleep close together for warmth," he explained to Wade. "Being the newest and strongest, you'll take the end of the row. It's a rule."

Wade looked at the row of men burrowing like animals in the sand. "What about blankets?" he said, dumfounded. "What about the tents?"

"Well, now those poor Secesh people hardly got enough blankets to send old General Beauregard," the gaunt man drawled. "And those tents are a wee bit overcrowded, being designed for twelve and housing thirty."

"But don't you ever get to sleep in one?"

The gaunt man shook his shaggy head and kept digging. "I've been here four months. The fellows in the tents came here long before me. There was a battle last year near the town of Manassas, by a stream called Bull Run. Everybody said it was going to decide the war, being the first battle. But it didn't. It only decided which Yanks were going to get to Belle Isle first and sleep in tents."

He stretched out a long arm and tugged Wade's trouser leg.

"Won't do any good standing there and feeling sorry for yourself," he admonished. "Lie down before all the best space is taken."

The warning hadn't been spoken too soon. A startling phenomenon was occurring. The prison pen seemed to be disappearing! The light-colored sandy spaces which existed while the men stood upright vanished rapidly as thousands of prisoners lay down for the night.

Wade forgot about the tents. In the emergency of insuring himself at least a plot to sleep upon, he dropped beside the gaunt man and scooped vigorously.

The older prisoner had worked himself into a comfortable position. "Fellow over in the next hundred has it all figured out," he said. "According to him when all the guests of this resort are stretched flat, there isn't but three feet by seven for every man."

The dimensions recalled the two graves dug for Otto Decker. "They give you more when you're dead," said Wade morosely.

The gaunt man did not reply. Wrapped in sand and barren night, he had fallen fast asleep.

## Chapter 6

# On the James

A SHRED OF PORK FAT SAILED OVER THE MOB OF STARVING Yank prisoners and plopped in the sand a yard from Wade. A second later a chunky man knocked down two rivals in the doglike scramble for it.

"Another week and I'll be like them," Wade thought, running his fingers through his hair, which, in two months on Belle Isle, had been singed to a frizzy copper-red.

Guards were tossing scraps from their mess into the stockade. They made a sport of it, crying, "Last piece! Last piece!"

Wade watched the scuffling through slitted eyes. He noted that the chunky man time and again used his speed to pounce upon a morsel first, or his strength to twist the prize from whoever beat him.

Several prisoners maintained their strength by drawing extra rations in return for working for the Rebs as clerks, carpenters, and blacksmiths; but the chunky man wasn't one of these. His skin was blackened by the weather. His clothing hung in rags. On the surface, he was like the ordinary prisoner who struggled to survive without special privileges. Like them, he should have been thin and tottering.

In the evening Wade spoke of him to his friend, the gaunt man.

"That'd be Paddy Riley. He's been eating for two. But all good things must come to an end, as the saying goes, and for Riley it ends tomorrow."

"I don't understand."

"A man named William Courtwright died three months ago. Nobody reported the death, because Riley drew his rations," explained the gaunt man. "Courtwright's name is down on the list with five hundred men being transferred to another prison tomorrow. There'll be no more food allotted him on Belle Isle, and Riley will be as weak as the rest of us in a month."

The gaunt man wriggled deeper into the sand. He mumbled, "G'night, boy," and soon was snoring.

Wade lay wide awake, musing with satisfaction on the justice about to overtake Riley. The loss of the extra rations so pleased Wade that it nearly blinded him to any other boon in the next day's transfer of prisoners.

Then all at once he was sitting up, wet with perspiration. He poked the gaunt man. "How do you know who goes out tomorrow?"

"You and me don't go out, boy."

"But how did you learn who does?"

"Morton down the line works for Major Turner as a clerk. He copied the transfer list in triplicate. You and me, we're not even on one copy. So go to sleep and quit fussing yourself."

Wade lay back in a little trance of excitement. The desire for sleep had scudded from him before a blow of fresh hope. While cooped on the island, he had no chance whatever of escaping the Rebs. But en route to another prison camp as William Courtwright, the man the Rebs didn't know had died, he might have many, many chances.

Tingling, he rolled in his hollow and peered across at Richmond. He wanted to reach out and rip the black sky on its spires and pointed roofs and flood the earth with daylight. He made himself lie quietly, but he couldn't relax. The radiant prospect of freedom alternated with the terrible certainty that he'd bungle everything at the last minute. Morning seemed to have lost its way, so slowly did the hours of night pass over Belle Isle.

At the faint, pearl-gray tints of dawn, Wade was up and doing. One shirtsleeve he tore at the elbow; his trousers he aged rapidly into rags; his face and skin wherever bare, he smeared with coal dust. When the five hundred men to be transferred lined up in rows of fours, he assumed the faltering gait typical of all old prisoners.

A Confederate captain and eight soldiers paraded smartly to the mid-point of the formation. A sergeant barked instructions, and then the captain read from a sheaf of papers. "Addams . . . Allan . . . Arling . . ." He bellowed the names in a foghorn voice.

To each name the designated prisoner answered, "Here,

sir!" and then shuffled from ranks and joined a new formation some dozen paces to the right.

The roll call droned through the A's and progressed
into the B's. Wade listened to the names above the wild
pumping of his heart.

"Butler . . . Cabot . . . Conners . . . *Courtwright.*"

Wade's throat tightened. "Here, sir!"

Even as he shouted, he would have given anything to
have the words back. For to the dead man's name three
other voices answered. Three prisoners besides himself
had perceived in the impersonation of William Courtwright the means of leaving Belle Isle.

The three broke from the formation in panic and
squirmed through the mass of onlooking prisoners. Despite fixed bayonets, the guards declined to pursue. A
thousand growling Yankees sealed the way.

Wade stood still, banking on the logic that the real William Courtwright would not run. The captain summoned
him and questioned him sharply. Wade replied without
hesitation. He knew the officer didn't want facts so much
as answers given the way the real Courtwright would give
them, calmly and confidently.

Age, birthplace, and sundry dates Wade invented on
the spot. He wouldn't remember what he had said five
minutes afterward, and neither, he judged, would the captain. What mattered was that the captain, who had no
way of confirming his answers, would believe him because of his sure and unfrightened manner.

The captain did. "Get in ranks," he ordered, and delivered a warning to any other prisoner who contemplated
substituting himself for a prisoner on the transfer list.

The calling of names resumed. When the last man had answered, the guards counted heads and started the column tramping at route step through the main gate.

Each man strode according to his own gait as the column wormed onto the hilly, grassy area where the prison personnel had their tents and shanties. The air tasted cleaner, and somehow the wind bit less cruelly here than in the prison pen below. Every gust, every blade of grass, every footfall held the whisper of freedom.

Wade's plan was to break away from the column as it went through the crowded streets of Richmond. But when the column stopped while still on the island, he changed his mind. He determined to bolt as quickly as possible.

For the captain in charge had been accosted by a tall young major. Neither the bandage which swathed the right side of the major's face from chin to ear, nor the sling which hid the three-fingered hand, could mask his identity. Wade dug his jaw into his breastbone, hunched his shoulders, and gazed sidelong at Roger Bragg.

The Rebel youth was reading the list of transferred prisoners with studious care. The captain held the sheets and flipped them at Bragg's nod. He read the first page again, then smacked it irritably with the back of his hand. The officers parted with a salute. The column was ordered into motion.

The ten seconds it took Wade to march past the scrutiny of the youth who hunted him to the death seemed like ten centuries. From the corner of his eye, Wade saw Bragg come closer and closer. Hunter and hunted came abreast, and for an agonizing moment all that separated them was a yard of brown grass and the changes wrought in Wade's appearance by two months of starvation rations and a thin layer of coal dust.

Then Roger Bragg was gone from view.

Wade felt as though he had walked through fire. He was out of danger, though hardly more than for a few days at best, a few hours at worst. Bragg would discover he was not in the stockade. If he delayed in attempting his escape, Bragg might even overtake the marching column. If the break failed . . .

The head of the column pounded onto the bridge which crossed to the mainland. Wade sprang from the formation and leaped.

He fell endlessly. Then his feet collided with a sheet of water the color of slate, and as hard. His knees jackknifed against his chest. He plunged through, and the river's piercing coldness surged around him.

He surfaced, blowing and gasping. Ramrods flashed on the bridge. Bullets screamed into the water around him, sprouting stalks of foam. He gulped air and dived.

He surfaced and dived again, and again. His ears felt close to bursting and his lungs burned oven hot before he would kick up. Each time, he took breath in a glancing, sharklike pass. Then he submerged into the deep, chill blackness once more, arms and legs flailing, body arching and flattening and straining.

Belle Isle and the bridge had receded into the distance when at last he looked back. He floated in mid-river gobbling the life-giving air. The current and his own efforts had borne him safely out of range of the Isle's artillery.

He had put Belle Isle behind him, but not danger. From Yanks who had tried to escape and been caught, he knew that Confederate pickets and home guards were posted on the shores. News of escaping prisoners was relayed through a rapid system of signal stations and couriers.

His one chance was in not repeating the error of the other prisoners who had succeeded in getting off the island only to be recaptured on the mainland. He had to avoid land until he had drifted beyond the tightly patrolled area around Richmond.

The current was at once his strongest ally and his most dreadful foe. It would carry him to safety or tug him under.

"Got to stay afloat!" he thought, splashing and gurgling.

He was not an efficient swimmer. His choppy technique suited well the small swimming holes of Kentucky, for which it was designed. The river extended for miles. The struggle to reach a point midway between its banks had taxed his muscles to their limit.

What was more critical, his hands and feet were slowly and steadily growing numb with cold.

Soon even the slight motions necessary to keep his chin above the surface tuckered him. Feet paddling in place, he cast about for something on which to rest. From the odd bits of lumber and refuse streaming by, he seized a narrow plank. It was inadequate to support his weight, and after swallowing a mouthful of water he quickly abandoned it.

Next a cask bobbed up, and spun away as his fingers laid hold of it. Fortunately, right behind drifted a fragment of a spar. It still wore strips of rigging, and these served Wade as handles. Clinging with both hands, he rode the spar downstream.

On either side the landscape spread level, and here and

there blossomed patches of May color. Presently gray soldiers appeared, running to the river's edge. Their muskets
rattled like a chain being dragged, and the water ahead
of Wade jumped whitely.

Wade ducked under the spar and emerged so that the
wood floated between him and the soldiers, forming a
kind of miniature breastwork. In so protecting himself
from one shore, however, he exposed himself to the other.

The soldiers' aim was remarkably inaccurate. Nor was
it improved upon by the five home guards who presently
rushed from among the trees on Wade's unprotected side.
They waged a fitful battle with their muskets, which misfired more often than not. When a shot did get off, the
ball invariably flew high and into the opposite shore.

The soldiers commenced to yell. The home guards
yelled back. Both groups claimed the other was coming
closer to wounding good Confederates than harming the
escaping Yankee.

During this heated crossfire of word and shot, Wade
held his raft to the center of the river. The zigzag flow
of the James made navigation, accomplished by scissor
kicks, extremely difficult. However, since the men on the
shore had demonstrated their inability to hit him, he was
able to devote all his energies to steering a course. The
water somehow felt less cold.

The gunfire from both banks continued, though without
the power to frighten him. The marksmen changed as he
drifted; cavalry, infantry, and civilians all took pot shots
at him. Every now and then a bullet ripped the water and
raised a tuft of spray within six feet of him, but never
closer.

The James swept him in a huge slithering rush. He had traveled some seven or eight miles when, from around a bend downstream, roared the heavy explosions of artillery.

Artillery bespoke a battle, and a battle meant hosts of men striving and scrambling back and forth. Wade envisioned the opportunity of gaining land unnoticed, in the confusion. He increased his speed by stroking with one hand.

Throughout the voyage he had made a practice of glancing upstream, because the Rebs, sooner or later, would launch boats, if merely to recover his body. He looked now, and what he saw turned him to redoubling his efforts.

Three small boats were in the chase. Their speed tripled his, and in a very few minutes they would overhaul him.

Everything depended on his attaining the thick of the battle before the men in the boats pulled him aboard, or slew him in the river.

He rounded the bend still ahead of his pursuers and was met by a great blur of hulls and sails. The river glittered under electric flashes. Thunderous booms clapped against the sky, and black smoke fringed a bout between giants. A flotilla of warships was dueling with the artillery of a Confederate fort embedded on a bluff two hundred feet above the water.

Before he had recovered from his astonishment, Wade was carried into a man-made reef of sunken vessels. He let go of the spar which had borne him so stoutly, and, swimming among partly submerged smoke funnels and masts, climbed into the top spokes of a paddle wheel.

The sunken vessels formed an impassable barrier directly under the fort. Obviously the Confederates had chosen

this site as the most strategic by which to close off the
river and safeguard Richmond from naval assault. Unless
the Union ships could first destroy the guns of the fort,
there was no chance of clearing the wrecks and steaming
up to the Rebel capital.

Perched as he was, Wade was trapped between two
perils: the naval bombardment and the three small boats
pursuing him. As these craft came into sharper focus, he
understood the disproportion of the perils.

Each small boat contained two men who labored at the
oars and a soldier who sat in the stern, musket on lap. In
the lead boat, standing in the prow, was a fourth figure.
He had one arm in a sling.

"You never give up!" Wade gasped.

A bullet whined, and wood splintered on a paddle above
him. Roger Bragg's boat was still a hundred yards upstream, but the Southern youth had begun using his pistol.

A bullet ripped wood, closer than before, as Wade
slipped back into the river. If he had to, he'd swim directly
through the spewing destruction of the warships. Not even
Roger Bragg would pursue him there!

The three boats came on steadily. They came in echelon
and each second they grew larger and Bragg's aim with
the pistol was better.

Wade watched them all the time. "Now the rifles," he
thought.

A soldier had risen from his seat in the stern as though
he meant to add the fire power of his rifle to Bragg's pistol.
Instead he screamed, *"The Monitor!"* The words, falling
into a sudden breach in the naval battle, carried clearly

to Wade. The effect upon the oarsmen was magnetic. They threw themselves around and gaped.

Bragg did his utmost to hold course. His scolding, his pistol-brandishing, his coaxing were to no avail. The oarsmen thrust their blades into the water, mutinously pulled the boats in a half circle, and rowed off the way they had come.

Unbelieving, Wade stared after them and then at the thing which had created such terror.

Creeping upstream was an amazing craft. What propelled it and what kept it afloat mystified Wade. It had neither sails nor smoke funnels nor paddle wheels. Its bare, iron-plated deck rested almost level with the river, as though it were too heavy, and sinking.

That the batteries on the bluff feared the monstrous vessel was evidenced by their concentration of fire upon it. No answering salvos roared out. The craft's two guns, set in a turret amidships, apparently could not be pointed to the height of the fort. Like a huge iron crocodile, the vessel swung around and nosed slowly back down the river.

While the guns of the fort were directed upon the ironsides, Wade swam for land. The river, his partner as long as he went its way, became a hard foe as he tried to cross it. The current pushed him with countless hands toward the boiling waters around the warships.

The shore line appeared a million strokes away. Gradually it drew nearer, and then he had arrived in water that reached to his waist. He stumbled in the shadows, lurched erect, and was knocked down by an undertow. He struggled and fought and reached dry ground. He fell down, sprawling, touching earth with his dripping forehead, and dragged himself inland toward the woods.

Branches parted. He swayed, seeking balance, awaiting whoever it was. A black face stared at him, wide-eyed, questioning, silent.

Wade tried to remember how it went. He recalled Luke and a rope ladder uncurling from a trap door overhead.

"L-light and loyalty," he stammered.

He had an instant to wonder if it would do any good. Then silvery shafts pierced his brain, and he slumped forward into the pit of unconsciousness.

## Chapter 7

# The Spy

WADE OPENED HIS EYES TO THE SQUALID INTERIOR OF A SLAVE
cabin. Through vision blurred by fever, he saw an aged
colored woman arise from his bedside. She wrung out a
cloth in a basin of water and gently dabbed his brow and
temples.

He slept, dreamed of his escape, woke, and slept again.
The hours and days sped by, marked for him by the fact
that sometimes the single room spun in light, sometimes
in dark. In time the fever lessened, and his head cleared;
and on the day the room stood still, Luke and a bull-
necked Irishman sat by the side of the bed.

"The grape-vine telegraph say a young gentleman climb
out of the James," said Luke. "I come quick as I can."

"How long have I been here?" asked Wade.

"Thirty-four days," said the stranger. He removed a card from his wallet. Wade reached for it and grimaced.

"Easy, lad," the man cautioned. "You're lucky to have that arm. It carried enough weight to sink a gunboat — a ball and three pieces of buckshot."

"I didn't know I'd been hit."

"You were too busy swimming," replied the stranger. His card identified him as William F. Meehan, an operative of the Pinkerton Detective Agency.

"Part of my job is to help Union soldiers return to their lines," he said. "Your case is different. I want you to *stay* in Virginia."

"Why?"

"Because you've got two things I like in a soldier, courage and ingenuity," replied Meehan. "My work keeps me in contact with the Loyal League; that's how I know Luke here. Through Luke, I learned about you, and especially about what happened in Otto Decker's barn."

"Then you also know I'm not the winner — yet," said Wade. "Roger Bragg, the officer I shot twice from a distance of two feet, is still very much alive."

"I know enough about you to want you in the secret service," said Meehan, rising. The tantalizing remark dangled in air as he set a bowler on his head and tapped it jauntily.

"We've talked too much for the first day," he said. "I'm due in Washington by Saturday. We'll chat again when I return. Right now, you need rest — all you can get. You've been a mighty sick young man."

How sick, Wade learned in convalescence. Besides the

wounds, he had contracted malaria, which, thriving on fatigue and undernourishment, had held him bedded for more than a month.

Through June and most of July, he recuperated in the slave quarters, hidden from the eyes of white men. His hospital was a log cabin, fourteen by fifteen feet square, vacated for his use by a family of six.

Luke told him the cabin was typical of most slave dwellings. The information shocked Wade. He never dreamed human beings could live in such poverty.

Thankfully, it was summer and warm, but the openings in the side, which passed as windows, and the loosely hung door suggested acute suffering from winter cold. In addition, a square hole of about eight inches had been cut for the purpose of letting the cat in and out. The one luxury was a deep impression, covered with boards, in the center of the earth floor wherein sweet potatoes were stored.

Sampling the primitive state in which slaves lived and died was not the only education given Wade.

From long talks with Luke he learned what the war meant to the Negro of the South. Although loyal to the white people in the "big house," even the most ignorant slaves on the plantation felt in their hearts that the freedom of their race would be the great outcome of the conflict if the Union armies triumphed.

Luke talked often of his hopes of becoming a free man. As the days unfolded into weeks, he stayed near Wade as helper, companion, and lookout; and the two youths swapped their dreams of life in a nation whole again and at peace. They reveled in the future and dodged the present, these two; the one, white, who was a soldier and no longer cared to be, the other, black, who wished to be a soldier and could not be.

In the last week of July Meehan returned.

"Sorry to be late," he apologized, as if he'd been gone six hours instead of six weeks. "I've been in Washington."

He laid a large parcel on the floor and placed his cane and bowler neatly upon the foot of the bed. His gaze followed Wade's nervous pacing with approval.

"Well?" demanded Wade.

"Well, my lad, you won't stay hidden much longer. I bring news, big news. Last Sunday, while riding to a funeral, Mr. Lincoln confided to Secretary Seward and Secretary Wells his intention of issuing a proclamation. The proclamation will declare all slaves free."

Luke regarded Meehan with an awestruck expression.

Wade gave a low whistle. "If the President frees the slaves, the Rebs won't ever quit fighting."

"At the moment, they are as far from quitting as a bear in a honeycomb," said Meehan. "Since Bull Run last year it has been one unbroken procession of victories for them."

"Reports reached us that General George McClellan's Union army was within seven miles of capturing Richmond on the last day of May," said Wade. "What happened?"

"Joe Johnston checked him at Fair Oaks," replied the detective. "Worse, Johnston was wounded in the battle — I say *worse* because his army went to Virginia's Robert E. Lee, the same Lee who refused the command of the Union forces to go Secesh with his state. Lee and that Stonewell Jackson mauled little Mac in seven days and chased him back down the peninsula to his warships at Malvern Hill. General John Pope has been called out of the west to take over the shambles."

"You make Lee and Jackson sound like men ten feet tall," chided Wade.

"They aren't, but they fight like they are," answered Meehan. "I'm not a military man, but I respect facts. The fact is, Lee has McClellan's number. And that fellow Jackson, though green as a corps commander, moves foot soldiers around like other generals do cavalry — fifteen, twenty miles a day. Maybe General Pope can lick 'em, but he never faced a team in the west like Lee and Jackson."

Wade said, "When you were here before, you spoke of the secret service. You haven't told me yet why you wanted me to stay in Virginia."

"Few man have the courage and strength to escape from Belle Isle," said Meehan. "That kind of feat recommends a man highly for work as a spy."

"I'm a soldier," asserted Wade, and glowered at Meehan, daring him to challenge the statement.

The detective tactfully declined. His observations were unnecessary. Wade himself had conceded the contradiction; he called himself a soldier and at the same time he wanted to retire from the war behind the mountains of Kentucky.

Meehan dealt directly with Wade's aversion to spying, an attitude common among soldiers.

"Of course," the detective said, "a soldier wears a uniform which protects him against hanging if he's captured. A spy has no protection but his wits. He operates within enemy lines, kills in self-defense only, and gathers no glory."

"You're being unfair," objected Wade. "I'm not after glory, and I'm not afraid —— "

"But you consider spying wrong — a form of deception not in accordance with a soldier's code?"

"Yes," answered Wade bluntly.

"I'm not ashamed of being a spy," said Meehan. "Right now the secret services have become more vital that ever. They must help bring about a victory in the field to give the President the opportunity of proclaiming the slaves free. Otherwise it might appear as our last shriek on the retreat, as Mr. Seward put it. And there's something else even more important."

"Go on."

"A Union victory now against Lee would halt England's threatened recognition of the Confederacy," Meehan continued. "The Confederate States are desperately trying to win acclaim abroad as a separate nation. If England extends Jefferson Davis's government official recognition, the other countries will follow her. The markets of the world will then be opened to the Southern purchasing agents, and everything the Confederacy cannot manufacture can be imported. Lee would at last control the materials to launch a full-scale offensive."

Wade envisioned Robert E. Lee at the helm of a magnificently equipped Southern army. It was a frightening prospect.

Meehan said, "The secret services can do their share in producing the Union victory Mr. Lincoln wants, and in preventing the foreign recognition he doesn't want. But we need more agents — young men like you to dig out information behind enemy lines."

Wade nibbled warily: "What am I to do about Roger Bragg? Attempt to take his place in the Southern army as he seeks to take mine in the Northern?"

"No," said Meehan. "I doubt if Bragg will ever catch up with you again. If he does, I'm banking on you. You will have to decide how to handle him. Once you walk into the Rebels' camp, you'll be strictly on your own."

Meehan had him hooked, and Wade felt himself being reeled in. He tugged feebly to break away. "Officially, I'm still on the muster roll of the Fifty-sixth Kentucky," he protested.

"You've been transferred to general headquarters, Army of Virginia," said Meehan. "I had you relieved of field duty in Washington four days ago."

"You were pretty doggone sure of landing me," scolded Wade, though unable to resent this methodical man who got what he went after.

"After Luke told me about hobnob in a hogshead and the escape from Belle Isle, I knew you were the kind of young soldier I wanted," said the detective. He broke the strings around the large parcel. "Your disguise. Sorry, no false whiskers."

Although lacking in this theatrical flourish, the parcel contained an otherwise complete wardrobe. A suit of butternut jean, a tall hat of beaver, a stout hickory walking stick, and a shoulder pack transformed Wade into a peddler of notions.

The masquerade had its note of irony, Wade reflected. He might still be serving with the Fifty-sixth except for another false peddler. Had not Roger Bragg, with pack on back, stopped at his Aunt Mae's cabin and seen his picture, Wade would now be doing the routine duties of an infantry sergeant. As a spy, he was unlimited in what he might do, provided he survived.

Meehan unbuckled the pack and spread out its contents: pins and needles and the trifling odds and ends which were in great demand by soldiers in the field and in garrison. He reviewed the cost of each article, and advised Wade the price to charge.

"Always overcharge," the detective counseled. "The experienced peddler is famed for his self-patriotism."

For the next five hours Meehan put Wade through a merciless briefing on geography, troops, officers, and the art of telling lies. It was late afternoon when he took up his cane and bowler.

"Start tonight," he said. "You have all the information I can give you. Good luck, peddler."

In shutting the cabin door after the detective, Wade had a sensation of somehow shutting a much larger door. A hateful chapter in his life as a soldier was closed. Gone were the days of flight, of running from Roger Bragg, Colonel Mapes, Otto Decker, and Belle Isle. He looked now to a future, however treacherous, wherein he moved at his own pace, and as his own master.

At dusk Luke helped him strap on his pack of notions.

"I guess I'll be going," said Wade awkwardly.

Luke nodded.

"I'll try my best," added Wade.

Still Luke said nothing. Wade knew how it must hurt him to watch another given the opportunity he'd have torn out an eye for.

"I'm sorry," said Wade.

Luke shook his head. "You do the best you can — and you got to do good. Ain't no one else I rather see go than you. You try for my people, Marster Wade."

The word "marster" was a stranger in the cabin. Wade understood that it had not just slipped in from long habit. It had been summoned. No more genuine compliment had ever been paid him.

A lump swelled in his throat. "I'll do my best, Luke."

From the plantation, Wade walked due south. Meehan had informed him that General Harvey Hill's headquarters for the Department of the South Side might be found in Petersburg. It was Meehan's opinion that Hill's Southern forces were there to keep guard on General McClellan's Northern giant, the Army of the Potomac, which sat licking its wounds at Harrison's Landing, across the James River from Petersburg.

Meehan's plan was for Wade to enlist in the Rebel army. The detective reasoned Wade would have better luck with a force in garrison, such as Hill's, than in joining regiments in the field.

By sustaining a rapid pace, Wade reached the Confederate camps outside Petersburg as the morning mist lifted in milky patches. Early though it was, the sentence of a court-martial was being carried out. Wade heard the strains of the Rogue's March. Some culprit was being drummed out of the service.

He headed in the direction of the music. At the edge of a broad field he saw a brigade drawn up in a square. Marching within the square was a mock procession: in front stepped a fife and drum corps; then came a file of guards holding their rifles upside down, and then a second file with bayonets fixed at the charge.

The prisoner marched behind the first file. His buttons had been snipped off, and the left side of his head and beard were shaved clean.

He was paraded until the officer in charge barked a command. The square broke apart, and a host of soldiers seized their former comrade-in-arms. They painted him with molasses and rolled him in the dirt.

Men from other outfits had hurried over to witness the fun. The prisoner became fair game, and many jumped into the sport of launching him out of camp with kicks, rocks, and clubs.

Wade circulated among the spectators. The disgraced man, he found out, had worked in headquarters under a Captain Davies, an assistant adjutant general, but excessive drunkenness had rendered him unfit for service.

Wade liked what he learned. If he were to dig up information of importance to the Union army, it would not be as an infantryman plugging in the ranks.

Opening his pack, he began to cry his wares. He sold five spools of thread and two packets of needles, and he worked his way toward a collection of wedge tents. Here the staff officers of the command were quartered; and here he would find Captain Davies, the officer who had just lost an assistant.

Wade shuffled in and out of the tents. The officers denounced him as a thief and a rascal for asking such prices, but he persevered, and at last came to the tent which bore the sign, *A. M. Davies, Capt., Ass't. Adj. Gen.*

Captain Davies was a slight man with abundant sandy hair, and, in Wade's opinion, rather too old for the rank of captain. He listened to Wade's pitch and he listened well. When Wade finished, the captain cut right to the point.

"What's your story, boy? You're big and strong. What are you doing peddling notions?"

"A man has to look out for himself in these times," said Wade, startled.

"You've been here before, haven't you?"

"No, sir, never," insisted Wade.

"Seems like I've seen you before somewhere."

"No sir," repeated Wade. If Davies happened to know Roger Bragg, the astonishing resemblance might lead to disastrous complications.

The officer frowned. The frown altered to the annoyed look imparted by a thought wiggling from memory. "Never mind," he said, and to Wade's relief embarked upon a new line of questioning. "You know what other youths your age are doing?"

"Yes, sir, and I'd like to be a soldier, too."

"Three weeks on the awkward squad would square those shoulders."

"I guess soldiering would help me," agreed Wade. "I tried to volunteer in '61, but I got this stiff left arm and the doctor said I'd be no good with a rifle."

"There are other things to do in an army. Can you read and write?"

"Yes, sir. My aunt taught me."

"Do you drink?"

"No, sir."

"That's in your favor. By curious fortune I'm in particular need of a clerk. My last one was drummed out of camp this morning because of an uncontrollable fondness for old red eye."

"I believe I noticed some such ceremony," said Wade innocently.

He thought the interview was progressing favorably. His first impression was that he liked Captain Davies, and he felt the officer liked him.

Davies' next question cracked like a command, as though Wade were already recruited and subject to military discipline. "What's your name and where are you from?"

Wade had decided beforehand to answer this question honestly, lest he be tripped later on the horns of a false name and a false abode.

"Wade Baxter, sir. I'm from Kentucky."

"A state of divided loyalties."

"Loyal regiments have been raised in Kentucky for the North and for the South."

Captain Davies' eyes narrowed speculatively. Shrewd wrinkles radiated from their corners. "Why do you want to be a soldier, Baxter?"

For an instant Wade felt that months had unpeeled and he was closeted in the hotel room in Clinton, answering questions of the citizens' committee. *Why are you fighting?* He didn't know all the answers then; he didn't know the issues of the rebellion, and he didn't know Luke. But now he had a reason for choosing to remain in the war instead of returning to Kentucky. And although he didn't answer as a Confederate, he answered honestly.

"Because I want to do God's will," he said.

For a long interval Captain Davies considered him without speaking. Then the officer said quietly, "You'll get on."

He scribbled on a piece of paper. "You can turn that pack of notions in to the quartermaster and get a receipt for it if you like. Draw equipment and rations from Sergeant Morgan. Anyone will direct you to him. Biggest man in camp. Give Morgan this note." He tore the paper in a clean rip. "Report here after evening roll call."

Wade flung up a hand in a crude salute. And as he departed Captain Davies' tent he looked beyond the Confederate camp toward whence he had come that morning.

"I'll do my best, Luke," he whispered. "I'll do my level best."

*Chapter 8*

# Secret Mission

WADE SPENT HIS FIRST DAY IN THE CONFEDERATE ARMY exercising his abilities as a spy. His success with Captain Davies bespoke his exceptional talent for the work. After reporting to Sergeant Morgan and drawing rations and a place to sleep, he set himself to inspecting the system of fortifications rising around Petersburg.

By evening he had amassed a headful of facts. These he intended to submit in person to General McClellan. As he strolled, he modestly accepted Little Mac's humble gratitude. He watched the Army of the Potomac crunching into Petersburg, wheeling to attack Richmond. He heard Wade Baxter being hailed by Mr. Lincoln as the savior of the nation.

94

It was a shock, therefore, when Captain Davies raved at him merely for being three minutes late. "I told you to be here at evening roll call. Where have you been?"

"G-getting my rations, like you said, sir," stammered Wade, "and just sort of getting acquainted."

Davies shook his head despairingly. "If you want to be a soldier, Baxter, you might try to obey orders. Especially mine, since I'm taking you on a mission tomorrow."

He examined Wade's peddler's attire critically. "You'll do, dressed as you are — the quartermaster is temporarily shy of uniforms. You may need a weapon, though." He fished a pistol and some cartridges and caps from a camp chest. "Don't go handling this like a spool of thread. Get Sergeant Morgan to show you how it disassembles — and be outside this tent by dawn."

In taking the gun, Wade purposely handled it like a spool of thread. But he made certain not to be late again. When, at daybreak, he stationed himself before the captain's tent, the area already bustled with horses and running men. A line of march formed rapidly. Captain Davies told Wade to board a wagon near the head of the train.

A little after seven o'clock an officer came spurring down the line, swatting his claybank mare with his hat and shouting, "Forward, boys! Forward!" Men yeowed, and to the tune of cracking whips and rumbling wheels the whole column jerked into motion and ground out of Petersburg.

"Where're we headed?" Wade asked the driver of his wagon in a tone he considered casual.

"Dunno," was the gruff answer. "Giddap, thar!"

If the objective of the mission was a secret, the column

entrusted to execute it was a downright mystery. Wade counted two brigades of infantry and six batteries — a force too cumbersomely weighted in artillery for a hit-run raid, and too lightly weighted for siege.

After it had traveled some seven miles, the formation dragged to a stop. Wade faced forward, and beheld a sawmill nestling on a rim of second-growth pines. Deeper in the woods glinted a strange crop which no mill blade could ever hew into balks and planks.

"You ever seen so much heavy stuff, boy?" the wagon driver asked.

Wade shook his head emphatically. The driver sucked his dry corncob. "Must be thirty-five field pieces and them two siege guns over yonder."

A ripple of excitement pulsed down the column. Somebody said Lee's own artillery chief, old General Pendleton, was in the mill.

"There go Harvey Hill and Sam French," the driver said, as two generals dismounted and entered the mill. He spoke of the high-ranking officers as a Northern soldier might refer to a pair of mess comrades.

The presence of Pendleton started rumors raging like brush fire. Something big was in the wind. The longer the conference inside the mill lasted, the wilder the rumors danced. Most of the men from General Hill's detachment had never seen so mighty an assembly of big guns.

The outcome of the conference shed no light upon the mission. There was a short advance of two miles. The column halted and the soldiers waited, fretting and grumbling. Toward midafternoon orders were issued: make fast the wagons, unload the caissons, rest the horses.

The driver of Wade's wagon hopped to the ground. He studied the landscape profoundly. His face beamed with a great and private knowledge. "By jiminy!" he exclaimed. "If we are where I think we are, we'll flatten McClellan's whole kit and caboodle!"

The chance to pry an explanation for these words vanished almost instantly. Captain Davies rode up, trailing a spare horse. He tossed the reins to Wade.

"Come along, Baxter. You've something to see today before it gets all spoiled," he said waggishly.

Davies went swinging off to a clump of high officers. Wade recognized the commanding general, Daniel Harvey Hill, a man of forty, who sat his horse restlessly and spoke with a white-bearded general Wade guessed to be Lee's man, Pendleton.

Hill took Davies' salute and briefly turned his intense eyes on Wade. Then the general lifted an arm in signal, and the little party moved at a silent trot through forest and field.

Presently Wade inhaled the odor of river wind so familiar from Belle Isle. Another moment and the officers broke through a file of trees and clattered upon a peninsula which curved into the waters of the James.

"Coggins Point," said Davies, smiling like a cat. "That's Harrison's Landing opposite us."

The riders had pulled up in the lee of the trees. For Wade the woods had parted upon a spectacle too gigantic to be taken in whole. It smote him in plots of color and patches of detail — a baseball game and men washing clothes, cavalry drilling and infantry drilling, and the whitecaps of tents sparkling in the sun. A thousand yards away sprawled the North's Army of the Potomac!

On the river before the encampments, stretching two miles in both directions, lay a vast fleet of ships, anchored and lolling like sleepy ducks.

General Hill lowered his telescope and spoke quietly. The gray hunters dispersed and ranged over the Point, seeking positions for their three-inch rifles, their howitzers, Parrotts, and Napoleons.

Wade rode beside Captain Davies, dazzled by this dreamlike situation in which he alone might save masses of the Union army from destruction.

His tongue was almost out of control against his teeth, but he managed to say, "It wouldn't take much to bring a Yank expedition swarming over, sir."

"Half a dozen pistol shots might do it, Baxter," replied the captain. His lips thinned in a twisting smile, and he peered up calmly into the sky where a Union observation balloon bounced on air. "I think that if anyone removed a weapon from its holster here, General Hill would personally shoot first and ask questions later."

Wade placed his hands in plain view by lapping them over the saddle pommel. He cleared his throat and said, "General Hill's got quite far from us, sir."

"So he has," said Captain Davies cheerfully. He nicked his mount with his heels, gently, the way a rider does who loves his horse.

Wade followed, sitting stiffly, positive that he had spoken when he shouldn't, that Captain Davies suspected him and that every officer on the Point had an eye turned on him.

The afternoon went badly for General Hill. By sundown only a small number of the stakes marking the placement of cannon had been driven down. The inaccessible terrain of Coggins Point perplexed the artillerists. Night had grown several hours old before the various units began to edge into position.

The delay had seriously impaired Hill's timing. The necessity for haste, plus an overcast which wrought uncommon darkness, resulted in widespread confusion. The generals consulted and agreed upon a day's postponement.

The command retreated into the shelter of the forest. The men complained loudly that the generals were lunkheads who had crippled their biggest gun, surprise. Yankee scouts would stumble upon them by morning.

To Wade the postponement meant hope. Yet in his heart he knew himself powerless to influence the result. Since he was now removed from Coggins Point, his shot, or a dozen of his shots, would not convey to the Union officers at Harrison's Landing the intelligence that seventy big guns were going to be pointed down their throats. Any attempt at warning would cost him his life.

He was sure Captain Davies peered at him from somewhere in the leafy darkness. He was almost disappointed to learn that the officer was with General Hill a mile away.

"Well, if no one's watching . . ." He immediately began to saunter through the forest. Once a major stopped him, demanding to know his unit. Once he had to help a sergeant untangle a prolonge. Within fifteen minutes, though, he had got to the rim of the trees.

The pickets were there, a tight chain of veterans, and

that was that. No one, colonel or private, was allowed to enter or leave the area. Utmost security obtained: no smoking, no fires.

The picture Wade had of himself as master spy and hero of the Union had been cracking and sliding all day. Suddenly it fell apart like a shattered mirror.

The role of spy had in his imagination appeared as the flint whereby miracles of havoc could be ignited with superb ease. In reality spying was blank aloneness. Night and the forest and Confederate pickets drove at him, husked him of his daydreams, and left him standing in trembling uselessness.

Not knowing what to do next, he trudged dejectedly to the wagon on which he'd ridden from Petersburg. The wavering light of a campfire flickered on his left. Odd . . .

"Appears like some of the boys want to stake us for the Yanks," he said.

The driver spat. "Not our boys. Irregulars. About eight of them come up this afternoon. Captain Etzwiler's fellas chased them with bayonets but they come back. Better sleep with your shoes on, boy."

Wade appreciated the advice. While with the Fifty-sixth Kentucky, he had seen bands of these "irregulars," outlaws who owed loyalty to neither side and fattened on the miseries of war. They plundered the dead of clothing and tracked the infantry for the booty of discarded equipment. They even bushwhacked stragglers, when they were short of arms.

Their fire burned in jeering defiance of the command. The silent bayonet attack had communicated something of extraordinary use. They camped and bided their moment, unafraid of these soldiers who refused to discharge their rifles or pursue beyond the wood.

"Vultures," said the wagon driver the next morning, as he scanned the ribbon of black smoke trailing from their embers. "They'll give us an audience tonight, and they'll clap thunderous loud for every man who falls with a pair of leather soles on his feet."

Wade dusted off a few Kentucky oaths for the benefit of the driver. Then he forgot the irregulars in grudging admiration of the men who had come to fight. Having given up all hope of escaping, he took a long, close look at the Rebel soldiers. And what he saw beneath the ragtag collection of uniforms stirred his esteem.

He had heard that these Rebs were the best fighters in the world, but, lacking discipline, the worst soldiers. A lie. Stalled helplessly in dense woods, with the mightiest army on earth lying at their feet, they cursed their generals, polished their weapons, and kept themselves in readiness. Seldom did they waste a glance at the sky, where the yellow eye of the Union balloon blinked here and there among the treetops.

It seemed outrageous to Wade that the balloon observer failed to detect them. He brooded over this, till he perceived that his idleness loomed large. Every officer and man had found some duty to occupy him. Wade pitched in wherever an extra hand was needed. He spent most of the long afternoon assisting the wagoners. He coated axles with lard to reduce squeaking, mended harnesses, and curried horses.

At four o'clock, rain began battering at the daylight. By six, when the orders were given, the column moved in semidarkness. The ground rolled treacherously; the wetted roads sucked at hoofs and wheels. Despite these handicaps, the guns were conducted forward in silence. A jubilant spirit ran through the men. David was stealing upon Goliath.

Wade and Captain Davies rode to Coggins Point to observe the distribution of the guns. The signal gun boomed promptly at midnight; then for an agonizing thirty minutes the generals withheld the bombardment until satisfied that all guns could fire together.

Along the opposite shore beads of lamplight glimmered pleasantly from shipboard. On the river and in the camps the stillness of sleep prevailed.

The stillness erupted at 12:30. Wade had the sensation of someone's opening a furnace door in his face. The night filled with ear-splitting roars, and flashes of horizontal flame. The ground quaked, staggering his horse again and again.

Occasionally three or four guns chanced to fire in unison. Then a great section of the Point was illuminated. Wade could see the cannoneers rapturously urging and feeding their monstrous pets. And like trained beasts, the guns bellowed out mouthfuls of death in horrible, blind obedience.

After fifteen minutes, the two guns foremost at the river's edge began to withdraw. Wade saw shells bursting on the Point. The men across the river had been stung to retaliation. From land batteries and gunboats the Union artillery blazed into action.

But by now the Confederate guns had fired their allotted rounds and were transported to the rear. Men and equipment burrowed deep into the night. The Union shells, screaming across the river, tore into Coggins Point and picked up turf and shrubs and splintered rock.

The Rebels had surprised McClellan in his den. They had bitten his heels and humiliated his reconnaissance. As Wade rode behind the singing artillerymen, he had difficulty in restraining his lips from their songs and his heart from their pride.

"Baxter!"

Wade twisted his torso in the saddle.

Captain Davies rode up like a fury. "Lieutenant Thurmond's gun overturned. C'mon!"

Together they galloped back through the rain and the roads of liquid mud. On the way Wade learned what the breakneck speed was all about. The band of irregulars had surprised Lieutenant Thurmond and his crew and routed them. General French wanted the gun recovered. Thirty infantrymen had been dispatched for the purpose.

After a mile's gallop they passed the gorge into which the gun had overturned. The gun wasn't there, nor were the irregulars. They were twenty yards farther on, and Wade and Captain Davies, going full tilt through the darkness, practically crashed on top of them.

A pair of the outlaws had started the gun in motion by sitting astride the terrified draft horses and whipping them ruthlessly. The six others of the band, absorbed in hurling stones at the mud-splattered haunches, did not immediately see the two soldiers.

Captain Davies yanked his stallion to a skidding halt. He brought up his pistol. Two shots unseated the riders, and roused a clap of musketry in return. Davies' horse fell;

Wade's, not so critically hit, bucked him off and plunged bleeding into the night.

Wade raced for the gorge, feeling the captain's breath on his neck. They hurtled over the craggy lip side by side, slid down the bank, and crouched at the bottom, winded and bathed in mud.

"Why didn't the infantry cover us?" Davies exclaimed. "Did you see any sign of them? Listen . . . Do you hear it? Skirmishing — to the right."

Wade listened. In the distance the Union cannons still pounded Coggins Point. The barrage exploded a million different noises.

"On the left," Wade contradicted uncertainly. "I think it's coming from the left, sir."

"Left or right, there's nothing to do but sit here and wait for our boys."

"Perhaps I could see, if I crawled up —— "

"No, you stay put," Davies snapped. He went himself, creeping warily up the slope. The Union barrage ceased as he climbed within a yard of the lip. He froze, listening for the sounds of the infantry.

There was nothing to hear now but rain.

"Look out!" Wade screamed.

A ragged man had sneaked over to the gorge. He ducked away at the cry.

Davies sloughed a path back down the bank, shaking his pistol. "Jammed," he gasped furiously. He tried to wipe the gun clean, but his hands and clothing oozed more mud over it. "What about yours?"

"Useless," said Wade. His pistol was barely discernible under the coating of muck.

"There must have been a change in orders. There isn't a sign yet of the infantry," snorted Captain Davies, leaving unsaid what his anger implied: that the infantry wasn't coming at all.

The ragged man reappeared at the top of the gorge. Davies shouted at him and raised his pistol. The man darted back, but Wade thought he saw teeth flash in a grin.

Davies saw the grin too. "They already suspect we're defenseless. We can't bluff them much longer."

Wade knew what the captain had in mind. Six to two were nice odds, especially if the outlaws deemed themselves safe from harm. Officers' uniforms brought a good price, and sidearms could always be dried and cleaned and polished like new.

"Too many months behind a desk has rashly whetted my appetite for adventure," said the captain. "Sorry to bring you in on this, Baxter. Funny, I wanted to see how you reacted to a little danger. Now I know, and it may be too late — "

"Look, sir," said Wade. "The gorge is V-shaped. Perhaps if we separated, and each got at one end, we might surprise them in the middle — the point. If they thought our guns *might* be working, they'd surrender."

"Under the circumstances, I'll try anything," said Captain Davies. "Don't show yourself till you hear me order them to lay down their arms. By heavens, we might just do it!"

They crawled in opposite directions, bellying in the mud to utilize the bottommost dregs of darkness. Wade reached his end and carefully scaled the bank. He peeked above the lip.

The six outlaws were advancing to the elbow of the V, where he and Captain Davies had crouched.

Wade cocked his useless pistol and prepared to stand. He had but a few moments in which to be scared. Then Captain Davies leaped boldly into sight of the outlaws.

"Lay down your guns!" the officer roared in his best parade ground voice.

"And throw up your hands!" Wade called, jumping up.

The startled men stared at the pistol in Davies' hand. Five of them lost their nerve and threw down their muskets rather than invite a crossfire. The sixth, the ragged man and by all odds the leader, called the bluff. He shot at Davies.

The ball gashed the officer below the knee. He limped over and smashed with the barrel of his pistol before the outlaw could reload.

"Collect their guns, Baxter," he said, panting.

Wade saluted, and across the senseless body of the fallen outlaw, Northern spy and Southern captain exchanged the long and secret smiles of two soldiers met in the proud fellowship of courage.

The capture of the outlaws and the recovery of the siege gun achieved more than a few days of glory for Wade. Captain Davies elevated him from the awkward squad within a week and placed him at a clerk's desk in general headquarters.

Wade did nothing more important than copy special orders at the company level, it was true. But he was in the converted schoolhouse when Lee's orders to General Hill arrived. Captain Davies and every officer present let go with a war whoop. General Hill was relieved of his departmental command and directed to rejoin his division in the field, taking with him his headquarters staff.

The Confederates were massing their strength for a campaign to relieve Richmond, and Wade would march with them. He should have felt joy equal to theirs over the coming battles, though for quite a different reason. In battle was the chance to strike the ultimate blow against them.

Yet joy was not among the emotions which the impending good fortune awoke in him. They were all so strange, his feelings, so unlike what he had expected.

For he had seen the Rebels' valor and determination close up, and he no longer found it easy to hate them.

## Chapter 9

# Four Cigars for Wade

GENERAL DANIEL HARVEY HILL LEFT PETERSBURG ON AUG-
UST 21 to join Robert E. Lee and the Army of Northern
Virginia. At Hanover Junction he picked up three of his
former brigades and McLaw's division, and thereafter he
drove straight northward, pausing at night to close up
stragglers and snatch rest. Before dawn, it was again
northward.

Wade rode as Captain Davies' orderly, because in the
field there was no place for him at headquarters. This
comedown from clerk to servant Wade regarded as a
mixed blessing.

Had he been returned to ranks as a rifleman, he would
not be in a position to come into anything of importance.

On the other hand, as a member of the officers' circle, he might suddenly find himself face to face with Roger Bragg.

As the force pushed up Virginia, the specter of Roger Bragg gradually faded. The fancied engagements of Wade's private contest with his relentless foe were churned into the makings of the great and real war. Wade, remembering the snap and dazzle of the Fifty-sixth Kentucky, was confounded by these Southern foot soldiers. They resembled more a horde of beggars than brigades marching to battle.

Besides their weapons, the men carried an oilcloth and a blanket on their shoulders and little else that was not absolutely essential. Tin cups, tied to the waist, had replaced canteens because of lightness. Overcoats were nonexistent, having been discarded the previous spring. The heat of the march now prompted the men to lighten further their burden by shedding articles of clothing they wished for in the chill of night. Some in every company trudged barefoot.

The nights were cold and getting colder. The men paired off for greater bodily warmth, pooling their blanket rolls. They slept shoulder to shoulder in the muffled dampness of the woods, one oilcloth on top and one on bottom. Between were the two blankets, sandwiching the men in with their lice and filth. But the men followed where Hill led, though it seemed to Wade the general was going to lead them into the streets of Washington.

He brought them close. The bedraggled brigades made camp on September 2 by the Little River Turnpike and discovered how close. A day's march due east would bring them to the hills overlooking the Union capital!

Toward noon a bunch of Georgia boys trooped over to

inspect the newcomers who had rushed all the way up Virginia only to miss the fun.

"Man, yuh missed it," they sympathized. "Yuh missed seein' them Yankees skedaddle!"

Before an hour elapsed, Hill's ranks were infiltrated by news walkers who recounted the Union defeats. Allowing two-thirds for exaggeration, the one-third left came up black and bloody: Lee had taught the Union's General Pope a murderous lesson in tactics.

While Hill had pressed to join Lee and the Army of Northern Virginia, the skillful Confederate chieftain had cut up the Union armies near Bull Run creek. In a two-day struggle the Yanks had suffered a worse licking than on the same spot thirteen months before. Another battle, or an extension of the one just fought at Bull Run, had been waged in a lashing thunderstorm on ground where Wade was now camped, and two Union generals had been slain. The last Union force had retired from the field but a few hours before.

Wade felt a bitter discouragement. Where was President Lincoln's long-sought victory, the percussion cap for the proclamation that the slaves must be freed? If these inspired Southerners could be led to victory after victory against the gigantic blue machine of the North, what hope was there?

"Stop dreaming, Baxter, and unload the tent."

Captain Davies had ridden up, heady with the atmosphere of victory and an overdose of port wine.

"Just the tent and chest," he said. "No, not the other wagon. We won't be here that long, boy. We're going after Yankees."

The normally tight-lipped little officer waxed talkative that evening. Wade listened as the captain spoke of the righteousness of the South's fight for freedom and the spirit of the Confederate soldier. He sprang up and down constantly, as hoppity as a rabbit. He had actually seen Lee and Jackson today! He had dined and wined with Mr. Turberville Stewart who lived in the big mansion Chantilly. "What a glorious day!"

Inevitably, the wizardry of the wine thawed in his blood. He grew serious, almost melancholy. "The price of victory was high, Baxter . . . nearly ten thousand casualties and five of our thirty-five generals wounded. 'Old Rawhide' Hill has filled up the ranks with fighters, though — every one worth three bluecoats. Wade Hampton's cavalry is up, and so is Pendleton's reserve artillery. We're going after Yankees, by heaven!"

Wade's ears rang that night. A truce, on Confederate terms, appeared likely. Three months ago he had first heard of Robert E. Lee from Detective Meehan. Then the Confederate capital was threatened by McClellan and his grand Army of the Potomac. In ninety days of command Lee had bottled McClellan in his own timidity and thrashed Pope. Now Washington, not Richmond, was faced with the threat of capture.

But it was not east to Washington that Lee sent Hill and his other commanders. It was north across the Potomac to the invasion of Union soil: to Maryland.

As the division progressed up Pleasant Valley toward Dranesville, Wade complained to Captain Davies. "We could take Washington. I don't understand going into Maryland at all."

Captain Davies laughed. "Don't be disappointed. Oh, we could capture Washington — at the cost of troops we can't replace. Then what? We wouldn't bag the government. Lincoln and his gang would flee to Pennsylvania and rally the abolitionists to greater fury than ever. No, sink a few sharp teeth into northern industries. Rip Yankee pocketbooks, and you'll see how fast those profiteers squeal for peace."

Wade nodded and rode like a faithful Reb, keeping his mouth shut and his eyes open.

Toward noon, General Hill peeled off Anderson's brigade with orders to discharge a few rounds into Yankee trains at Berlin. With the brigades of Colquitt and Ripley, he pushed on to the mouth of the Monocacy, deftly routed a small contingent of Federals, and crossed the Potomac into Maryland.

It was here that the first link in a strange and momentous chain of events was forged. Once across the Potomac, the division was thought to be nearer to Stonewall Jackson than to Lee. The order embarking Hill upon the Maryland campaign had been signed by Lee's adjutant, Colonel R. H. Chilton. Was the division to continue to receive its orders from Lee, or from Stonewall? Convention suggested the former, expediency the latter.

The question occurred to Captain Davies. He inquired of his superior, Major Ratchford. Since it seemed simpler to reach Jackson, Ratchford directed Davies to have Stonewall resolve the riddle. Thus while the division remained at the Monocacy destroying the lock and the canal banks, Wade and Captain Davies galloped after Stonewall.

Two blind men might have followed the trail. The appearance in Maryland of Jackson's three Confederate divisions could scarcely escape notice. It was, however, the general's departure from character which stamped the crossing so memorably. In a rare dramatic caper, he had whipped off his hat and waved it while yet in the middle of White's Ford. A band played "Maryland, My Maryland," and the soldiers responded by singing and sounding the Rebel yell.

"It was a sight to behold, I tell you," said the long-winded old farmer who supplied each detail lovingly. "Some citizen gave Ol' Stonewall a gray mare and he took it with thanks. Said his little sorrel had been stolen, and the claybank he was riding didn't suit him much. Somebody else gave him a melon, and ——"

"Where is he now?" interrupted Captain Davies.

The old farmer seemed offended by the captain's impatience. "Well, I don't rightly know," he said huffily. "Reckon down that road a piece."

A long piece. Dusk had gathered by the time they overtook Jackson near Frederick, a town about eight miles from where he had crossed the Potomac. When finally they got past his pickets, the general had retired for the night.

"We better not awaken him. The matter can be settled in the morning," advised Captain Davies.

Although they arose early in the morning, Jackson had arisen earlier. Arriving at his tent, they witnessed the general preparing to mount a large gray mare.

"Is that Jackson?" demanded Wade in a hoarse whisper,

somehow finding it incredible that this man in a plain gray uniform and mangy flat cap was the dreaded Stonewall.

Captain Davies murmured assent. Wade stared as Jackson fitted his foot in the stirrup. So commonplace an action shocked Wade. It snipped at the legends being woven about the man. Jackson should have surged upward, blending with his horse and making one living instrument of grace and strength.

The horse shied. Jackson was compelled to hop thrice after it before he pulled his boot from the stirrup. He said something to the orderly holding the bridle. Then amused and grinning at the little difficulty, he prepared to mount again.

"The horse doesn't know the general," whispered Captain Davies. "It must be the animal he received yesterday as a gift."

Jackson had got astride and was sitting the big mare with the mastery of a born horseman. He talked to the animal but she was either ill-trained or deaf and did not start. He tapped her lightly with his spurs. With a harsh scream of rebellion, she reared upright and to the horror of the onlooking officers plunged over backwards.

By a miracle, Jackson was thrown clear. He tried to rise but could not. Reluctantly he submitted himself to the care of his aides. An ambulance was fetched, and half an hour later the general had recovered sufficiently to be removed from the ground.

"He's hurt his back," Captain Davies told Wade after consulting one of the attending surgeons. "A painful injury, but not serious, thank the Lord."

"Did you speak to him, sir?"

"On an administrative technicality while he's lying on the ground?" asked Captain Davies. "Of course not, Baxter. He'd have had me arrested. General Hill ought to be arriving with the division tonight. He can always get his brother-in-law's ear."

"I didn't know General Hill and General Jackson were related," said Wade in surprise. After a pause: "I don't suppose it's easy for General Hill, especially being the older man."

"You mean he's jealous of General Jackson's rank and fame?" The idea seemed to have been offered Captain Davies for the first time, and he mused upon it. "Well, now, I imagine he can't help but be envious, in a way. Still, it's not our right to argue whether he is or isn't. We'd better saddle the horses. We'll ride with the wagons till General Hill arrives."

The officer and youth walked to the meadow where the horses foraged, assuming the answer to the question of paper authority over Hill's independent division would be obtained later by Hill himself. Since Lee and his chief lieutenant, Jackson, functioned in close compact, the worst that might happen was that Hill received the same order from both. Where was the mischief in an extra copy, except perhaps to the bookkeeping of the adjutant's office? What possible harm . . .

"Baxter," said Captain Davies suddenly. "Look there. Those fools are tormenting the poor beast!"

A circle of soldiers had formed in the meadow about the gray mare which had unseated Jackson. The animal bleated in pain, and her eyes shone red with rage and terror.

Four ropes bound her shanks and stretched her to a cruelly wide-legged stance. A short fifth rope forced her head down to within inches of the grass.

"She's done us more damage than all the Yank generals together," bawled one soldier, who was vengefully clubbing a stout branch across the bleeding loins.

"We oughta find that fellow who gave her to Stonewall!"

"Yeah, and tie him under her belly and gallop him all the way to New England!"

"Hey, lookit Dackow."

"Go fix her, Joey boy!"

A rangy man smoking a cigar and wearing a comic stovepipe hat had come near to the horse. He held a queer harness, which he raised and lowered in front of him with delicate pleasure, like an executioner enjoying the weight and balance of his ax.

"That's an odd-looking rig," said Captain Davies as he and Wade entered the circle. "What do you make of it?"

The straps and hobbles recalled a similar harness Wade had seen used years before in Kentucky on an outlaw stallion. "He's going to truss up the mare," said Wade. "He'll tie her and let her fight herself out. She'll be better off dead when he's done."

The man with the branch had yielded his place to the man with the more subtle and entertaining method of punishment. Dackow fussed with his contraption, spreading it out on the ground and sorting out the ropes and straps and rings. When he had arranged the thing to his liking, he began to fasten each piece to the mare. This required about five minutes. He said nothing to anyone, though he murmured softly to the animal.

"All set," he said, and, over his shoulder, "cut the legs free."

The four ropes were slashed by eager volunteers. Immediately the powerful mare attempted to rear, but the rope at her head thwarted her. Half crazed, she repeated the action with redoubled effort. Dackow observed patiently, and then yanked at a strap, pulling her forelegs from under her. She plunged forward and fell onto her knees.

The crowd of soldiers shouted, and Dackow acknowledged their approval by tipping his hat. Dancing lightly out of danger, he threw the mare again and again. From each fall she struggled up more weakly, her breath rattling in her throat. The rope at her head had become a needless safeguard.

"Cut that rope," called Dackow, his voice high with excitement.

"How long does this go on?" Captain Davies demanded of Wade.

"An hour, an hour and a half if the horse is exceptionally strong and full of spirit."

Dackow jerked a whip out of his belt and unfurled it with a *crack!* "Cut that rope," he repeated.

Captain Davies stepped forth. "Let go of it, soldier," he said to the man who had stooped to Dackow's bidding. "You've had your fun, the pack of you. Now go back to your companies and leave this animal in peace."

Dackow went rigid. He turned slowly and regarded Captain Davies, a look of sly innocence on his sallow, lean face. "Why, captain, this here is a loyal Union horse. This here horse like to kill General Jackson."

"I know very well he threw the general."

"We got to tame this here horse, captain. We got to make doggone positive this here horse don't ever act up again."

"That isn't the way to tame a horse!"

"No?" inquired Dackow, his eyes lifting in wonder. "Could anyone break this here big critter by *ridin'* her, sir?"

It was a challenge insolently thrown. The other soldiers snickered at the unknown officer who had fallen into Dackow's trap. For to tame the mare by riding her must in effect belittle Jackson's horsemanship: it was a rash officer who willingly rode the horse Stonewall Jackson could not ride. Smugly Dackow touched his hat and propped the cigar between his teeth.

Captain Davies flushed. "Take your damned contraption off and put a bridle on," he snapped. "I'll break her."

The cigar nearly fell from Dackow's lips. He glanced for moral support at the crowd of men who seconds earlier had cheered him. They edged off, sobered by this little gamecock of a captain. And Wade, peering at Davies, seemed to see him truly for the first time.

A thin, undersized man who would never lead a charge, he none the less had a quiet daring. It was not the common, brain-wiped fearlessness of the battlefield, but the rare inner courage to follow his conscience.

"He's the only officer in the meadow," Wade realized. "The others don't want any part of this."

Unquestionably the mare had been abandoned to the

anger of the men. Their leaders did not care to deny sport
to troops already acutely reduced by desertion. The mare
was a burnt offering for co-operation when co-operation
counted, in the stress of battle.

Dackow removed the harness and slipped on the bridle.
"She's all yours, captain," he taunted, blowing a jet of
cigar smoke. "General Jackson ain't gonna pin no medal
on you. Seems to me you're a good bet for a stretcher."

The taunt stung Davies, and he said icily, "How good
a bet?"

Dackow faltered. He had used a figure of speech, and
Captain Davies had speared him on it. He wiggled off defiantly. "Anything you want to bet, captain."

"My saber."

"Agin what?" Dackow's voice was tight, suspicious.

"That smells like a first-class Havana. Have you any
more?"

"Four more."

"That's the bet, then. Your four cigars against my sword,
soldier. Baxter, come here and hold the stakes."

Dumfounded, Wade obeyed. Absurdly, fantastically un-
even stakes, he thought. Then he comprehended. Captain
Davies would have wagered against the mud on Dackow's
shoes. Not the cigars but Dackow's unchallenged brutality
as a horse tamer was the stake.

Captain Davies approached the mare. He stopped by
her head, full in her view, and looked into her red-glaring
eyes. Her ears were laid back, and her teeth showed. He
talked, and presently the ears relaxed, the lips uncurled
and met.

He stepped nearer, very carefully and slowly, and laid his hand on her forehead. He continued gentling her, winning her, restoring her faith in man.

He removed his spurs and untied the rope which bound her by the neck. The animal trembled, hunching backward in an odd, nervous crouch, ready to bolt at any half-seen movement. Captain Davies made none till he was ready. He appeared to be studying the broken flesh on her back, estimating the degree of pain his weight would cause on the bleeding surface.

He gathered the reins in his small hand. Then quickly he was astride.

The mare gave no sign, other than a twitching of nostrils, that she felt the rider. "Perhaps," thought Wade, "she will not buck at all." He envisioned her starting as easily as a Virginia walking horse.

These were momentary thoughts. With one tremendous buck leap the big gray soared into the air. She slammed to earth in a jarring crash, and the contest was on. Up and down the mare sprang, twisting and writhing, rearing high and whirling and bucking and whirling again — and always that terrible smash to the ground on four stiff legs.

It did not appear to Wade that anything could live on that horse. Side bets were being wagered around him on the number of minutes and seconds the man could survive. The issue was not whether the man could tame the beast, but how long the man would try.

The bucks increased in violence. Captain Davies bled at the nose. Soon he had lost co-ordination with the motion of the horse; his body began to flap exhaustedly.

"He's goin'!" came a shout, and suddenly the soldiers,

forgetting how they had wagered, cheered the man on as one voice.

The end came all at once, and hardly as foreseen. The mare plummeted from the sky; her hoofs dug into the earth and she held fast, as if asking for a truce.

"Get off!" cried Wade. About him the cry resounded loudly and urgently.

Captain Davies refused the dangling honor of a draw. His heels kicked in, goading a renewal of the contest.

Then and there the big gray, her flanks heaving and her coat discolored by sweat and blood, surrendered. Her mane tossed once in a farewell to freedom. She lifted her hoofs daintily and set them on a gait of the most gentle rocking. As if she knew it must some day be so, but had waited for the right hand, she responded with a joyful obedience. She trotted, cut right and left, galloped a quarter mile, and raced to a dirt-spraying halt ten feet from Wade.

A score of soldiers rushed to catch her reins.

"Easy with her!" Captain Davies panted, his concern that of a soldier toward a brave and noble foe.

He dismounted wearily. The flesh around his eyes was puffed and blackened, and he dabbed at his bleeding nose with a handkerchief. He said, "Give me my saber."

Wade extended the weapon. Captain Davies drew it from the scabbard and strode on Dackow. Calmly, efficiently, the blade hacked until the contraption of straps and ropes lay ruined, and with it Dackow's reputation.

Captain Davies smiled serenely. "Come along, Baxter."

As they strolled across the meadow, Wade said, "You forgot your cigars, sir."

"Cigars?" Captain Davies frowned. "Oh, Dackow's — keep them for yourself," he answered, and with the same serene smile added, "I don't smoke."

Wade didn't smoke either, but it seemed wrong to confess this and conclude a perfect morning on a negative note. So he kept the cigars.

"I'll give them away," he thought idly.

Three days later he was to leave three of them for a soldier he neither knew nor saw. As a result, the September wind sighed for days over thousands of unburied dead.

### Chapter 10

# Special Orders No. 191

WADE HAD HARDLY GOT COMFORTABLE IN THE SADDLE WHEN
Captain Davies cried, "Whoa-oa-a!" He dismounted and
strode rapidly into an oak grove.

In the grove were several tents and more generals than
Wade had ever seen in his life. "Two rounds of canister
fired smack in the middle of those tents would end the
war," he thought.

Captain Davies was gone briefly. "Our division arrived
late last night and is camped a mile to the south," he said
upon his return.

"Did you find out anything about who is to give us orders, sir?" asked Wade.

"No," answered Davies. "I didn't get to speak with any

of them, though they're all in there — Lee, Jackson, Longstreet, and Hill. General Hill has taken over General Jackson's corps till Jackson recovers, and he's got enough to
do without my bothering him."

"What do we do now, sir?"

"Ride back to the division. I wish I'd never started on
this, Baxter. If orders come down from both Lee and Jackson, we simply will have to start a 'duplicate' file."

They rode back to the division, which had pitched its
tents and located its kitchens. The Army of Northern Virginia needed rest, and Lee settled his men into a tranquil,
baselike existence for four days.

Soon the petticoat brigade descended from town and
farm. Young lieutenants and captains received the inspiration of a dainty handclasp and a coy flutter of eyelashes.
Lucky indeed was the officer above the rank of captain
who possessed good looks and youth besides. His ration:
a hug, a kiss, and a wildly enthusiastic entreaty to perform
deathless deeds against the wicked Yankees.

The men in ranks fared less well. The welcome which
Maryland offered them had to be stolen. Lee had posted
guards around Frederick to protect the town from hungry
sergeants, corporals, and privates. But he apparently re-
signed himself to feeding his army without a commissary;
hence the land became fair game. Wade foraged as hungrily as anyone in fields of green corn, in apple orchards,
and in hen coops. Daily, farmers stormed into divisional
headquarters, denouncing the Army of Northern Virginia
as a blight, a pack of unwashed chicken thieves, and a
plague of scavengers.

"If you will only understand," Captain Davies would plead. "Please, if you will only help us, we will help Maryland be free."

His apologies carried more force on September 8. On that date Lee issued a public statement to all Marylanders, formally explaining the presence and purpose of the Confederate army.

The statement, a dignified and friendly appeal for secession, began:

". . . The people of the Confederate States have long watched with deepest sympathy the wrongs and outrages that have been inflicted upon the citizens of a commonwealth allied to the States of the South by the strongest social, political, and commercial ties."

Lee proposed to cast off the Northern yoke, though leaving it up to the Marylanders to decide their destiny. The statement concluded:

"This army will respect your choice, whatever it may be; and while the Southern people will rejoice to welcome you to your natural position among them, they will only welcome you when you come of your free will."

"Is General Lee attempting to woo Maryland or conquer it?" asked Wade.

"Both," answered Captain Davies. "Maryland has shown a strong inclination toward the South since the beginning of the war. Moreover, it nearly surrounds Washington, and if we can win the state without shedding blood —— "

A black horse smashed to a stop as though it had struck a brick wall a foot in front of Captain Davies. The circus stunt and the envelope between the rider's teeth certified him as a member of that dare-devil class of army horse-men, the dispatch rider. He yanked the envelope and grin-ned. "General Hill's headquarters?"

"Yes," replied Captain Davies. "Give it here — I'm the adjutant."

"From General Jackson, captain."

Captain Davies swiftly signed the receipt and tore open the envelope as the dispatch rider raced off. "In Jackson's own hand," he mumbled.

He crumpled the envelope and strode inside the head-quarters tent. "Baxter, I want you to deliver this."

After enclosing the dispatch in a fresh envelope, which he sealed, he scribbled across the front: "Original opened — Davies." To discourage tampering, he marked his ini-tials on the back where the flap sealed.

"You'll find General Hill over at Best's Grove," he in-formed Wade.

The youth pinned the envelope inside his shirt. Once out of sight, he slowed his horse to a walk. The envelope had begun to sting his chest. Was it important? If he could unseal it and peek . . .

Captain Davies' initials frustrated that idea. Wade dared not gamble, yet.

At Best's Grove a sentry told him that General Hill had ridden into Frederick. Lacking a pass to town, Wade re-ported back to Captain Davies. The officer had mounted, ready to deliver the dispatch himself, when Wade spoke up quickly. "May I go along, sir? I'd like to see the city."

Davies consented, and for a while they rode in silence through the camps. The officer surveyed the units sprawled around them, his face strangely pinched.

"Don't be disheartened by what you see, Baxter," he said. "Eighty years ago George Washington's army must have appeared as ragged and hungry."

"Desertions have hurt us," Wade remarked quietly.

"General Lee still has fifty thousand." Captain Davies moved his breast in a sigh. "True, our division has lost some men — mostly ones from the mountain districts of North Carolina. A lot of them hate slavery. They joined up to defend their homes, not to invade the Union."

Wade felt called upon to voice his contempt of the Union armies. "We'll whip the Yankees for good the next time we meet them," he said, parroting the campfire boasts.

"I'm afraid it won't be that easy." Captain Davies' face wore the iron look Wade had seen once before, at the taming of the gray mare. The look was one of determination not to be bested, regardless of the odds.

"The North," thought Wade, "will need all its men and equipment if the Rebs can field many more like this skinny little captain."

Upon entering Frederick, Wade obtained permission to stay an hour and explore the city. General Hill was readily located on the street, chatting with three brigadiers; and while Captain Davies delivered the dispatch, Wade led his horse into a nearby alley.

The mount's health being perfect and his trappings comfortably fitted, Wade had to manufacture an excuse for remaining within earshot. He examined the uncomplaining animal for nasal gleet, strangles, worms, and rheumatism. He deliberately turned his back on the group of officers; whatever comments the message might draw could be of no interest to an orderly.

Minutes passed. Wade fingered the animal's coat and thought: "General Hill must have opened and read it long ago."

He heard neither comments nor orders. Shuffling around the horse, he faced the officers.

General Hill stood alone; Captain Davies and the three brigadiers were walking out of view to the right. Hill was studying the dispatch, his body slightly stooped, his face set in utmost concentration.

"He can't be reading this long . . ." thought Wade, puzzled. Then he realized the paper must bear information so crucial General Hill was *memorizing* it.

As Wade watched, General Hill folded the dispatch and lifted his gaze. Quickly the youth bent over his mount's forehoof. He examined it blankly. When he peered up again, the part of the street visible from the alley was deserted.

Except that on the spot where General Hill had been standing lay a sheet of paper.

Wade edged to the building line and glanced up and down the street. It was untrafficked save for two rosy-cheeked girls of about six. They meandered over the road, arm in arm, warbling a squeaky singsong:

> We'll rally round the flag
> Boys, we'll rally once again
> Shouting the battle cry of Freedom.

A breeze cuffed the paper and twisted it several inches. Wade lumbered onto the street, looking like a harmless blunderer who had lost his drill mates.

The paper fluttered. By the merest lengthening of his
stride he pinioned it securely under one big foot. He
knelt as if to tie his shoelace and the paper vanished off
the street.

> The Union forever,
> Hurray! boys, Hurrah!
> Down with the traitor, up with the star . . .

The warbling died as the two small Unionists stared uncertainly at the tall, awkward figure in his shabby peddler's garb.

"Which side are you on, mister?" they asked together.

Wade walked toward the alley. The two inquisitors tagged along, chanting their one question relentlessly.

"I'm a soldier of the Confederate States of America," he
said, squeezing out a smile. "Now run along to Mommy."

"A Reb, a Reb, a Johnny Reb!" they chorused, and
manned positions for a fresh assault of verse.

> Down with the traitor, up with the star;
> While we rally round the flag, boys, rally once again
> Shouting the battle cry of Freedom!

There was no escaping. The alley backed into a gateless
fence. The way to the street was blocked by the two little
songbirds. What they lacked in size they made up double
in stubbornness. Arms linked and mouths a-chirp, they
stood pudgily determined to sing themselves hoarse on
the spot.

Inasmuch as he could neither ride past them nor over

them, Wade used his horse as a shield and unfolded the paper.

One glance sufficed. He read the scrawled handwriting with heart slugging against his ribs.

Hd. qrs. A. N. Va.
Sept 9, 1862

Spe. order
    191

III   The army will resume its march tomorrow taking the Hagerstown road. Genl. Jackson's command will form the advance & after passing Middletown with such portions as he may select, take the route toward Sharpsburg cross the Potomac at the most convenient point and by Friday morning take possession of the B & O R.R. capture such of the enemy as may attempt to escape from Harpers Ferry.

IV   Genl. Longstreets command will pursue the main road as far as Boonsboro, where it will halt with reserve supply and baggage trains of this army.

V   Genl. McLaws with his own division and that of Genl. R. H. Anderson will follow Genl. Longstreet & on reaching Middletown will take the route to Harpers Ferry & by Friday morning possess himself of the Maryland Heights & endeavor to capture the —

Wade stopped reading to turn the sheet over and draw breath. "Good God!" he thought. "It's Jackson's order!" Trembling he read further:

— enemy at Harpers Ferry and vicinity.

VI   Genl. Walker with his division, after accomplishing the object in which he is now engaged will cross the Potomac at Cheeks Ford, ascend its right bank to Lovettsville take possession of Loudoun heights if practicable by Friday morning, Key's Ford on his left and the road between the end of the mountain and the Potomac on his right. He will as far as practicable co-operate with Genl. McLaws & Genl. Jackson in intercepting the retreat of the enemy.

VII   Genl. D. H. Hill's division will form the rear guard of the army, pursuing the road taken by the main body. The reserve art. ordnance & supply trains etc will precede Genl. Hill.

"Good-by, you old Reb," one of the girls called. They had apparently grown disgusted. This man wasn't worth teasing. He didn't do anything like a soldier; he merely stood statue-like, a piece of paper in his hand.

Wade heard them skipping off, warbling in duet.

> The Union forever,
> Hurray! boys, Hurrah!

The way to the street — the way to the Union armies — lay clear. Yet, Wade could not take it till he had finished. Hypnotized, he read the last part:

VIII   Genl. Stuart will detach a squadron of cavly to accompany the commands of Genls Longstreet, Jackson & McLaws & with the main body of the cavly will cover the route of the army & bring up all straglers that may have been left behind.

IX   The commands of Genls Jackson, McLaws & Walker after accomplishing the objects for which they have been detached will join the main body of the army at Boonsboro or Hagerstown.

X   Each Regt. in the march will habitually carry its axes in the Regt. ordnance wagons for the use of the men at their encampments to procure wood etc.

By command of Genl. R. E. Lee
R. H. Chilton
A. A. Genl.

Most of the names and places listed were unknown to Wade. But one fact came howling up at him: *this was the master plan of the Confederate Army for the next several days!*

As the paralysis of shock wore off, he scanned the paper again. Not only did the order disclose the vital information that the Rebs were dividing their army; it gave precise details on the lines of march, the objectives, the positions of the supply train and cavalry, the location of the rear guard, and the place where the detached units were to reform.

If this paper, authenticated by Jackson's handwriting, could be conveyed to the Union generals, the separate Reb commands could be struck one by one and annihilated. The war would be over in two weeks!

The most unbelievable part of it all was Hill's dropping of the order. Was it deliberate?

Wade reread the sentences relating to Jackson. Stonewall was to capture the arsenal at Harpers Ferry, to pour new glory into a cup already running over; while Hill, the unsung brother-in-law, had the dry and dusty assignment of guarding the rear.

Had General Hill thrown the paper to the street in a fit of jealous temper?

"Baxter!" Captain Davies — a frantic Captain Davies — spoke at the top of his voice. "General Hill has lost the dispatch. Have you seen it? Did anyone pass on this road in the last few minutes?"

"Two young girls, sir. I haven't noticed anyone else."

"If those children picked it up!" Captain Davies looked

about desperately. "If those children . . . What's the matter with you?"

Too late to hide the paper. Captain Davies was staring.

Wade pulled his hand from behind his hip. "I found this on the street," he said, barely above a whisper. "Is it what you're hunting for?"

Captain Davies seized the paper. A fleeting glance and he gasped, "Thank the Lord!" and went running down the street.

Wade leaned against his horse. Had he attempted to stand by himself, he most certainly would have fallen. He felt weakened and rent by the opposing personalities within him.

To Wade Baxter the Union spy, the yielding of the order was an unpardonable sin. He should have bolted past Captain Davies — slain him if necessary.

To Wade Baxter the Rebel orderly, the cold-blooded killing of Captain Davies was unthinkable. Further, the knowledge that the order had been accidentally dropped vindicated his opinion of the Southerner as a fighting man. General Hill had not been guilty of jealousy.

He mounted his horse and rode slowly back to camp. Only then, as he viewed what he had done from a distance, did he understand it and himself fully. As a soldier he would kill as the creed of war demanded. But neither as a Yankee nor a Rebel would he be the instrument whereby tens of thousands marched to certain death. That was the job of the generals.

"I wonder how generals do it," he reflected grimly.

Captain Davies overtook him outside the town. The officer was jubilant.

"Baxter, you've done a service to the Confederacy today," he said heartily. "There are a lot of folk in Frederick who would trade an arm to carry that order to McClellan."

Wade did not know how to reply. He made conversation from a scrap. "McClellan, sir? Isn't General Pope the new Union commander in the east?"

"Not since the second battle at Manassas," replied Captain Davies. "Pope has been sent back to the West where he can try to forget Robert E. Lee. News of it arrived yesterday. McClellan has been given a second chance at leading the armies in the East."

Wade grinned, as though this latest scrambling of Union generals thoroughly delighted him. But he thought: "Won't President Lincoln ever find *one* general with the courage and skill to match the Southern leaders?"

Out loud he commented: "Old Abe must be at his wits' end to clutch onto McClellan. General Lee has beaten him, and will again whenever they meet. The Yankees must realize that."

"They haven't much of a selection," said Captain Davies happily. "McClellan will need a miracle to stop us."

"A *second* miracle," thought Wade. The first had been rejected in a Frederick alley; the likelihood of a second seemed as remote as the sun exploding.

The sun did not explode. But the second miracle, in the shape of a dispatch rider, was pacing restlessly by General Hill's vacant tent.

"What is it, soldier?" hailed Captain Davies.

"From General Lee, sir."

Captain Davies' gaze roved over the dispatch too rapidly to be reading. "Do you recognize this?" he asked, handing it to Wade.

Wade saw the first two paragraphs. "Why, it's a copy of the order General Hill dropped in Frederick."

"No, it's the original; the other was the copy," corrected Captain Davies. "What I expected has happened. General Lee has sent originals of the order to his corps commanders, and to our independent division. Obviously, General Jackson considers us part of his corps, and to be certain General Hill was informed of tomorrow's movement, wrote out a copy for him."

Davies opened a knapsack wherein he stored papers of no immediate importance.

"Our duplicate file, Baxter," he announced. "Since General Hill already possesses General Jackson's copy of the order, we can put this one away. Let's hope the file never outgrows a knapsack."

During the remainder of the day Wade played hard at having no feelings. Still, there were moments when the gray troops around him refused to co-operate in his game of toy figures. They joked and swore and talked of home like human beings.

"Pick out any three," he thought, "and two will be dead within a week if —"

At night he wrapped himself in his blanket and oilcloth, bundling air-tight as though to imprison both his body and his mind. It was useless. His thoughts drifted unerringly to the miracle in the knapsack . . . to the filed-and-forgotten order no one would ever bother with till the war ended and the army of historians relieved the army of fighters.

He had watched the sun go down, and, sleepless, he watched it rise. The camps awoke in a vast movement of men, horses, supplies, artillery.

As usual, he assisted in loading the headquarters' wagon. He made a special point of carrying out Captain Davies' knapsack.

And when no one was looking, he reached in and stole Special Orders No. 191.

## Chapter 11

# "Now I Know What To Do!"

"Hurry up there, Baxter! Do you want to be left behind?"

As he shouted, Captain Davies pivoted his horse and soon became engulfed in the stream of men and horses sweeping across the meadow.

Wade stood as if moored. Around him the gray tide drained from the ground where it had rested four days. Men with tattered shirts tramped by him. Men with shoes bound in rags, and men with neither shoes nor rags.

They sang. Rollicking tunes were shuffled from regiment to regiment. The weak and the cowardly had fallen away like husks, and to Wade the tough core of fighters left seemed unconquerable.

They sang though they had no wagons laden with salt pork and flour and honey. They must live off green corn and chestnuts and apples. They must live off the land, and their voices swelled, because the land beneath their feet was Northern land. For seventeen months theirs had been a war of self-defense on the Confederate soil of Virginia. Now they were carrying the taste of grape and canister, Minié ball and bayonet, to the peoples of the North.

The songs faded. The tattered singers etched into the landscape, forming a column miles long and becoming, by the magic of distance, the fearsome Army of Northern Virginia.

Alone with his horse, Wade slipped the order from his pocket.

*"Ride with it to Washington,"* thought the Union spy.

"Pretend you never saw the order," the Confederate orderly countered.

The temptation to heed the orderly was overwhelming. It was the easy way out.

"Why me?" thought Wade, tortured by his own wavering. The decision, because of its terrible responsibility, because of its enormous consequences, because it might shorten the war but doom thousands to their graves — the decision belonged to the generals to make. "Why must *I* decide?"

His hand on the sheet of paper had become clammy damp. He writhed as though inside him spy and orderly strove in a physical struggle for mastery. The struggle might have eventuated in a deadlock, had not a voice from his memory — from his memory and his conscience — settled the matter.

"You do the best you can, and you got to do good . . . You try for my people, Marster Wade."

Wade ceased to writhe. He laid the order on the ground.

"This is my best, Luke," he whispered.

He had started for his horse when a small detachment of soldiers galloped from a grove and headed straight for him. The leader, a colonel, gruffly demanded to know what he thought he was doing.

"Checking the area for anything that might have been left behind by mistake, sir," lied Wade. "I was told to."

"Find anything?"

"No, sir."

The colonel eyed him distrustfully. Wade guessed the horsemen were from the provost marshal, assigned the job of policing the evacuated camps for laggards and deserters. He remembered the four cigars which Captain Davies had given him and dug one from his saddlebag.

"I did find a cigar, sir." He smiled ruefully. "I don't smoke."

The colonel accepted the cigar. His tone softened. "You better catch up with your unit. Anybody go *that* way?"

"I didn't see anyone, sir. They all fell in, as far as I know."

The colonel chewed the cigar and peered down at the ground — at the order which had blown close to the front leg of his horse.

Wade breathed again as the colonel shifted his gaze out to the meadow. Everywhere the grass was scarred by the black, oblong patches of fire sites. Strewn near and far were the leavings of an Army. A pack of rickety hounds snooped and sniffed among chicken bones, hog bones, corncobs, boxes, and empty flour barrels.

"We'll rate Hill excellent on stragglers and pretty bad on sanitation," the colonel pronounced with dry humor. "Who's next?"

"Walker's area, colonel," one of the soldiers said.

"Let's have a look. You, son, get back to your command."

Wade saluted and put his foot in the stirrup. But as soon as the soldiers had ridden from view, he walked to the order and picked it up. The colonel had seen it but had taken no heed.

Special Orders No. 191 would never be found if abandoned as an anonymous scrap of paper among the trash of the meadow. This solid fact wedged between Wade's desire to serve the Union, and his reluctance to bear the terrifying brunt of responsibility. He searched for a middle course: a way to insure the finding of the order and yet hoodwink his conscience. If he could free himself from the guilt of dooming thousands of Rebels, and yet inflict upon them a major defeat, and so shorten the war . . .

He did the one thing he could. He baited the order. Carefully wrapping the paper around the remaining three cigars, he laid the packet on a level stretch of prominent ground. Then he fled the meadow at a gallop.

All that day and the next he lost himself in the march. The division shepherded the wagons northwest from Frederick. Laboriously the wheels turned by Middletown and through a low pass in South Mountain called Turner's Gap.

"Put ten thousand men in that pass and you plug up

the range tight enough to hold back the whole Union army," said Captain Davies.

"We don't have ten thousand men," said Wade.

"You're forgetting Longstreet's corps up ahead," answered the captain.

But Longstreet's corps was not destined to be up ahead much longer. There had been rumors. The Yankees under McClellan were said to be moving toward Hagerstown, Lee's designated advance base. And right or wrong, the rumors carried weight with General Lee. When the gray column entered Boonsborough, Longstreet continued on to Hagerstown, thirteen miles away, to get a toehold before the Yanks arrived, and to secure whatever provisions were there.

Behind him the forty-five hundred troops of Daniel Harvey Hill sat down to guard the vast parks of wagons and reserve artillery spread around Boonsborough. Wade saw a great deal of Hill that day and the next. The general was on his horse and going, as might a man who needs watch two directions at once.

Hill concentrated mainly on the roads leading north from Harpers Ferry. The danger from that direction was the twelve thousand Yanks of the garrison who might flee Jackson's assault rather than submit to capture. But occasionally Old Rawhide looked backward, toward the east, where McClellan's army might come piling through the hole in the mountains at Turner's Gap.

Wade looked much at the mountains, and at himself. Whatever he felt for the Rebs — and it was soldierly admiration for tough and spirited warriors — he told himself he had accomplished his work as a spy and fulfilled his promise to Luke. He had done his best. The past two days with the Rebels had been the momentum of habit.

Turner's Gap was the door leading back to his rightful part in the war.

At dusk he began to reconnoiter the pickets encircling Boonsborough, and before a new dawn he was riding. He traveled rapidly. Night veiled a way which nevertheless was easy to follow. He had marked every mile of it in coming, as if he'd known his masquerade as Reb would end at Boonsborough.

In six months he had traveled numberless roads, as sergeant, jinx, prisoner, spy, and orderly. Now all roads merged; and all roads led, like gathered strings, to a meadow outside Frederick.

Shortly before eight in the morning he rode within sight of the town, and within sight of a six-man Union patrol. Wade raised his hands when ordered. To protest here was foolish. Let them think him a Confederate deserter.

"The sweat on your horse tells an interestin' story, like about fifteen miles between us and the Rebs," the sergeant in charge said shrewdly. "You got a story as good as your horse's?"

Wade shook his head. His story was good — too good for the ears of a sergeant. He allowed himself to be disarmed and escorted into Frederick.

The town had undergone a startling transformation. The buildings, the grass, the trees, the dirt roads all seemed stained a Federal blue.

He turned to the sergeant in astonishment.

"Surprised?" the sergeant asked, chuckling. "The ad-

vance units arrived yesterday. The main body is comin'
up right about now. Ninety thousand soldiers can recolor
the whole earth, eh, Reb?"

Wade gaped at the mass of bluecoats creeping and shim-
mering and spilling like a swarm of locusts into field and
gully and forest. Once safely in town, he spoke up.

"Take me to your commanding officer," he said. "I have
important information!"

The patrol had halted by a high building. The sergeant
dismounted and slapped Wade's leg. "Inside, Johnny," he
said, "and cool your heels."

"But I demand to see your commanding officer — "

"You heard me. Inside!"

Wade was hauled to the ground and roughly cast into
a small, high-ceilinged room. The door slammed and
locked. He had a flashing vision of the order being picked
up by a Union soldier, ripped open, and tossed to the
winds in favor of the three cigars. He banged his shoulder
against the door and pounded with both fists.

Eventually he saw the uselessness of persisting. He
looked around for means of breaking out. His prison, a
storeroom of sorts, had one window. He reached it by
piling crates one on top of another. The window was too
narrow for him to squirm through, but upon thrusting his
head out he glimpsed an object which made his heart leap:
a red-on-white battle flag bearing the familiar goldenrod
emblem and beneath, "56th U.S.V."

He jumped down and beat on the door. He beat till
voices sounded irritably.

The lock turned. A blond, smooth-shaven captain and
one of the soldiers of the patrol confronted him.

"What's all the noise about, Reb?"

"I'm not a Reb," said Wade, as calmly as he could. "I'm a Federal soldier — a sergeant in the Fifty-sixth Kentucky Volunteers, or used to be. That's my old regiment two hundred yards away."

The captain peered at the ladder of crates banked to the window. He smiled knowingly.

"I can prove what I say," insisted Wade.

"You've proved that a Reb with good eyes, a familiarity with Union battle flags, and a little imagination can clap together a useful tale."

"We were in the fighting around the Bethels last year!"

"Indeed? So was I," replied the captain. "Tell me, soldier, which New York regiments were engaged?"

Wade had to rake his memory, but only for a moment. "The First and Second New York."

"There was a major killed trying to turn the Confederate left. His name?"

"M-major . . . Winthrop, sir."

"Who commanded?"

"General Pierce."

The captain squinted at Wade, knitting his brows with the air of a man studying an oddity through a magnifying glass. "I don't know," he muttered. "I don't know . . . but I'm going to find out. Fall in, and no tricks."

Wade fell into step, though it was a strain to keep from running recklessly ahead. As they marched across the field, he suddenly faltered. Suppose none of his former comrades recognized him? Or suppose they didn't want to recognize the "Jinx"!

He scanned the camp for his old tentmate, Tom Watson. He looked for a slight, boyish figure in a sergeant's uniform, and he didn't see one. He didn't see anyone he knew. The faces everywhere were the faces of total strangers.

He felt panic. "Where's Company A?" he asked shrilly, seizing a soldier by the arm.

"Leggo," the man growled. "This is Company A."

"Wade!"

Tom calling, and Tom — Lieutenant Tom Watson — dashing over, his arms waving, his face alight with surprise and joy.

Wade spun, threw up his arms, and the two old friends embraced wildly. The blond captain observed the reunion for a minute. Then he ambled back to his duties, grumbling about fool scouts who captured their own people rather than report in empty-handed.

"*Lieutenant* Watson!" Wade gasped, recovering his breath. "When did it happen?"

Tom grinned. "Two weeks ago. Jackson hit us, and there wasn't an officer in the company who escaped without a wound. The regiment lost so heavily they had to cork us with a battalion from a Vermont outfit. Say — " he stepped back. "Speaking of uniforms, where on earth did you get that rig?"

"That's too long a story," rejoined Wade. "Right now I have to recover a piece of paper, an order from General Lee to General D. H. Hill."

And with the words tumbling onto each other, he related how he had stolen the order and planted it in the meadow.

"Do you think you can find the spot?"

"Can I? I took my bearings like a sea captain!"

"Well, why are we standing here talking!"

As they cut across the bivouacs at a half-run, Wade quoted the order as best he could. Tom became visibly more and more excited.

He also did some calculations. "The order was dated the ninth of September, and this is the thirteenth. If I have any concept of troop movements, McLaws is fifteen miles off our left at Maryland Heights. Hill is at Boonsborough, fifteen miles off our right. Longstreet is fortifying Hagerstown. Walker is headed for Loudon Heights. Jackson is marching between Martinsburg and Harpers Ferry, forty or fifty miles from anybody. Good Lord, Wade, the Reb army is split into five parts, and three parts are too far away to support those nearest us. We've got 'em at last!"

"*If* we recover the order," declared Wade.

"Don't worry," asserted Tom. "If it's gone, the chance is good that a loyal Northerner picked it up. The important thing is that someone in army headquarters recognizes Jackson's handwriting."

"Hey, you've got it wrong," said Wade. "The order isn't in Jackson's hand. It's in Colonel Chilton's."

"What?"

"I told you. The order I gave back was a copy, which Jackson made for General Hill. Hill has it now. The order we're looking for is one of the originals Colonel Chilton wrote for General Lee and apparently had delivered to all the top commanders of the Reb army."

Tom slowed, evidently upset. "Then it's worthless."

"I don't understand you," objected Wade.

"General Headquarters won't believe the order in a million years," stated Tom.

"Why not?"

"Because Chilton is an obscure colonel. How many Federal officers ever heard of the man, do you suppose? Ten? Five? How many do you imagine can remember his signature well enough to verify it on the order? Why, I couldn't even be positive of yours. Do you see? The order will be regarded as a hoax, as a faked document deliberately left behind to mislead us."

Wade felt dazed, stupefied. Never had it occurred to him that the order might not be believed; or, rather, that it would be treated as an ingenious ruse.

He moved as in a dream past great hordes of soldiers, past stacks of arms and pots of fragrantly boiling coffee.

"How much farther?" inquired Tom.

Wade came alert. They were in the meadow. "On top of that rise," he stammered.

"I don't see any paper," said Tom. "I don't see anything but a lot of brown grass. You're sure it's the spot?"

"Yes," said Wade. "Maybe . . . a little left."

The two youths walked to the left, then to the right, then back and forth.

"You're certain no one saw you lay it down?"

"I'm certain."

"Well, it's gone."

"Wait," muttered Wade. "There were a lot of hound dogs snooping . . ."

"I never saw a dog that fancied cigars, for smoking or chewing," quipped Tom. "I've heard of bloodhounds and foxhounds and wolfhounds, but never tobaccohounds. Of course, if there was such a creature, he'd probably be a chewin' critter, say a spitz."

"You're a big help."

"I hate to be dogmatic," Tom teased, "but are you quite sure you didn't dream this?"

"You know better than that. Somebody found the order. Maybe somebody who recognized its importance and carried it to the Rebs."

"It's a cinch no Union man found it or things would be popping around here," said Tom, serious again.

"Perhaps they are," said Wade. "What do you make of him?" He pointed to a colonel galloping through the bivouac.

Tom whistled. "That's the fastest riding colonel in the Union army."

Suddenly a boy of about thirteen, lugging a drum only slightly larger than himself, lurched within arm's length, and Wade seized him.

"Who is that officer — the one on horseback?"

"Colonel Colgrove," the startled boy answered, peering over the top of the drum. "This is his regiment, the Twenty-seventh Indiana Volunteers."

"Does he always ride like the Johnnies are breathing down his neck?" questioned Tom.

"I guess it's 'cause the Johnnies is givin' up," said the boy. "I hear tell Private Mitchell and Sergeant Bloss of Company F found a box of cigars, and inside was a copy of a note Lee was fixin' to send General McClellan askin' for peace."

"His story tops yours, Wade," said Tom, smiling. "Surrender!"

"Some stories improve with retelling, but not mine," rejoined Wade, and released the little drummer. The boy headed for a group of soldiers gathering about two of their comrades. Wade and Tom exchanged quick looks and followed on the double.

As they drew near, Wade saw that the two men at the hub of the commotion were a first sergeant and a private. He guessed them to be Bloss and Mitchell, and he sought to force his way in. About a hundred others had the identical idea.

"Pull your rank, lieutenant," he urged Tom.

Tom bellowed, "Give way, there!" When absolutely no way was given, he lowered his head and went in at a charge. When he reappeared, he was minus his cap, but beaming.

"Those two found the order," he said, adjusting his rumpled uniform. "Colonel Colgrove has taken it to General Williams, the division commander. If the general puts any stock in it, he'll go straight to General Headquarters." Tom gestured at a group of tents close beside the city limits. "That's where we ought to be."

They went at a lope. While still quite far from the tents, Wade observed the abnormally large size of the headquarters population, both civilian and military.

"Seems like the news has already reached there," he said.

"You've been a Reb too long," answered Tom cynically. "General McClellan is not exactly the bashful kind. He doesn't discourage an audience."

Wade understood the remark before very long. While
Tom stationed himself at one end of the row of tents,
Wade watched the approaches from the other. Soon he
began to wonder. Would the order be welcomed as the
means of shortening the war, or darkly resented for the
same reason? Peace would disband this international court
of self-seekers.

The chatter of the court filled Wade with numbing
anger. There were disgruntled officers who sought commands, bewhiskered politicians and spotless journalists
who fancied themselves master strategists. There were
dainty men in elaborate uniforms who spoke with foreign
accents, and flabby profiteers who fawned after contracts
ranging from horses to shoelaces. General Headquarters,
under the proprietorship of George B. McClellan, was a
grab bag of personal favors and special privileges.

Into this lair of misfits, malcontents, and fortune hunters
rode a man in tweedy brown. Wade, on the lookout for an
officer bearing Special Orders No. 191, gave the civilian
but a passing glance. Yet the newcomer was so unob-
trusive as to be striking.

The youth watched in edgy curiosity. The man strolled
through the area, engaging in conversation with various
groups. Always he managed to disengage himself with a
gracious smile and a well-oiled bow.

"An educated listener," thought Wade, and just then
Tom came running up.

"The order has arrived," he shouted. "It's certain to be
taken to General McClellan."

"Somebody did recognize Colonel Chilton's signature
after all," Wade exclaimed.

"Colonel Colgrove brought the order to division head-quarters while Colonel Pittman was on duty. Pittman is the divisional adjutant, and, incredibly, he knew Chilton in Detroit before the war. He's in that tent now convincing McClellan's staff that the signature is really Chilton's."

"Will they believe him?"

"It looks like they have," said Tom.

Two colonels and two generals had stopped before the largest of the headquarters tents. The flaps parted, and a short man emerged. He greeted the officers with a grave nod. His manner was heavy and studied in every line, like an emperor who is inwardly supremely confident, yet who must appear humble before the populace.

McClellan's appearance had been noted. Still none among his courtiers ascribed any exceptional significance to the little council in front of his tent. Wade and Tom were able to drift within a few feet of the officers. So, too, was the man in brown.

McClellan held the orders in his right hand. "Pittman confirms this?"

"He does, sir," said a colonel.

The general stared at the order again. Suddenly he threw up both hands like a man grown tall enough to tear down the sky. "Now I know what to do!" he cried out.

The cry electrified the court, and all heads snapped about. McClellan seemed mortified by his exhibition. He strode hastily into the tent.

A great buzz of speculation arose in his wake. Only the man in brown acted with any knowledge of what had transpired. He untied his horse, leaped into the saddle, and whipped the animal out of camp.

"Lee will learn the orders have been found," mumbled Wade helplessly.

"Huh?" grunted Tom.

"That man in brown. I'll bet my life he's carrying the news to the Rebs. Lee ought to know by tonight or early tomorrow morning."

Tom marked the receding horseman. "It won't make any difference," he said. "The Confederate forces are already committed. And I doubt if Lee will alter his plans radically on the say-so of one private citizen."

Tom's words restored Wade's spirits. What mattered above all else was that McClellan had the order.

They walked to the camp of the Fifty-sixth. Behind them was a man who possessed the mightiest advantage over an enemy ever granted a military leader. By means of a piece of paper, he wielded the power of a god.

The man was George B. McClellan, master organizer and genius of preparation. It remained to be seen whether he would now move his armies like the god of battle or the god of the dress review.

### Chapter 12

# Burnside's Bridge

McClellan started boldly. Within an hour of reading
Special Orders No. 191 he had the Northern army moving
in pursuit of Lee.

Wade barely had time to report to his old regiment
and, aided by Tom, to make the outward change from
Rebel to Yankee. He drew a uniform and fittings, a breech-
loader and forty rounds of ammunition, and three days'
cooked rations. The ready supply of food and equipment
amazed him. After weeks with the impoverished Southerners, he was awed by such plenty.

Once in motion, the army clogged every westward road
for the span of miles. As Wade mounted a summit and
viewed the enormous, creeping rectangle of bluecoats, he

experienced a sense of unreality. The year before he had fought in the battles around the Bethels. Now he realized these were puny scuffles between regiments.

Here was order and deadly purpose on an earthshaking scale. Along the flanks and at the front ranged the cavalry, feeling ahead and protecting the sides. Layered inward was the infantry, and next the artillery. The defenseless wagons — forty feet from the tip of the leading mule's nose to the studs on the tail gate — lumbered safely over the innermost roads. Strung in the rear and gradually unraveling came untested recruits, stragglers slowed by fear or exhaustion, convalescents, special-duty men, and washing women. Last of all and hurrying to catch up were foragers who had been out plundering chicken coops and hog pens when their regiments broke camp.

The very bigness of the army begot snags. No one had prepared the land for ninety thousand travelers, and the roads bedeviled the many lines of advance. Not only were these country roads too narrow to permit more than four abreast with passing room left over, but they curved and joined and crossed maddeningly. Units which arrived first at a junction had the right of way; the others dispersed into the fields, stacked arms, boiled coffee, and lost time.

These enforced breaks waxed more rigid as the day waned. The men were made to stand at order arms at the roadside, ready to move at a moment's notice.

"We're getting close to 'em," said Tom. "Captains have begun riding up and down this column like errand boys."

"We still have to get to South Mountain before we

make contact with as much as a division," answered Wade.

Presently signs of the enemy appeared. The swollen body of a dead Reb, pinned beneath the carcass of his horse, evidenced a clash between opposing scouts. The shuttling procession of captains increased, and the men in Wade's regiment began to grow tense and quiet.

"There'll be a fight before dawn," he thought. He was positive that McClellan would speedily cross South Mountain and fall upon the Rebs, crushing them piecemeal before they united their divided forces. He was flabbergasted, therefore, when an order was given to leave the road and make bivouac.

He complained to Tom. "McClellan knows where the Rebs are. Why doesn't he push on instead of losing precious hours here?"

"McClellan is the commander in chief," said Tom.

"But Harvey Hill has less than five thousand men at Boonsborough. He couldn't hold Turner's Gap for a wink if this army decided to ram through South Mountain."

"You're forgetting you know more than McClellan does," said Tom. "According to Special Orders No. 191, Longstreet is with Hill at Boonsborough, near enough to hold Turner's Gap with its natural advantage to the defenders. How can McClellan divine that Lee has revised the order and sent Longstreet's corps on to Hagerstown, and that Longstreet's corps can't possibly have got back yet? I don't question that Longstreet is racing to reinforce Hill this minute. Even so, the Rebs will have to stretch their ranks pretty thin. Turner's Gap isn't the only way through South Mountain, though the National Road makes it the logical choice. Our Sixth Corps has already moved south to breach the passes there."

"A lot of good men are going to die on that mountain," said Wade.

Tom's head jerked around. "A lot of good Yankees, perhaps. There are no good Rebs." He nudged Wade's arm. "See you in the morning," he said, his tone a trifle too formal, and he departed for the officers' area.

During the early hours of night the word "jinx" cropped up. Nothing came of it, however. By daylight Wade was marching through the lovely valley of Middletown and the voices of war began to drown the mutterings of superstition.

Uneasily the men looked ahead, from whence sounded the splatter of muskets and the infrequent belching of howitzers. Five miles away South Mountain towered distinctly in the focus of the sun. Barrels glinted and puffs of firing winked on and off like fireflies, tinier than the tiniest pinpoint.

The distance made all motion but the flashing of light imperceptible. The column was halted and the men of the Fifty-sixth waited by the road like spectators queuing for tickets to a theatrical. For an hour the mountain disclosed nothing but its somber, gray-green side, inlaid with a lacing of white stone walls.

By-and-by the entrails of battle oozed out. A trickling of Union wounded came first. Most of them had minor hurts and wore temporary bandages. As they walked to the hospitals at the rear they exchanged banter with the troops along the roadside. They were obviously not displeased to be going away from the mountain.

After three o'clock Rebel prisoners plodded in a parade of misery. A barefooted man, his head and throat swathed in bloody strips of muslin, staggered quite close to Wade. He suddenly tore off his bandages and waved them at the sky like banners. He seemed to be trying to speak someone's name. His eyes enlarged and fixed in disbelief on the glaring sun. Then his arms fell, his mouth opened in a rent of loneliness and woe, and he collapsed into the dust of the road.

One of his comrades hoisted the dead soldier onto his back. Not being a strong man, he was compelled after covering a hundred yards to deposit his burden, which for all his care slid head foremost down the short bank of the roadway.

The body still lay unburied the next morning, eyes sightless and staring, ears deaf to the silence on South Mountain. The gunfire and killing had ceased. The Rebs had been driven back during the night. McClellan had wrested a victory!

The spirit of triumph prevailed among the men of the Fifty-sixth as they set to the tasks of burying the dead, assisting the wounded, and reclaiming the equipment strewn about the fields.

One soldier knew the victory to be an illusion. Having knowledge of Special Orders 191, Wade understood the Rebels' tactics at South Mountain. By waging a delaying action, Lee had gained life. He had held the passes long enough to save his trains of artillery and supplies. Somewhere beyond the mountain he was collecting his scattered army for a stand.

All that day of September 15, the popularity of General George B. McClellan climbed steadily. At twilight, however, it received a jolt. News reached the ranks that Stonewall Jackson had that morning captured the Union arsenal at Harpers Ferry and its garrison of twelve thousand men. Only a small command of Union cavalry had dared and made good an escape.

The men grumbled and eventually voiced their complaints openly. If Jackson and his corps had been eighteen miles away at Harpers Ferry, what kind of victory had really been won at South Mountain? Now, while the regiment used litters and shovels instead of rifles, Jackson was surely bringing his veteran foot cavalry up to rejoin Lee at a high-tail gallop. Why didn't McClellan pour his mighty hosts through the mountains, swamp Lee, and then meet and destroy Jackson en route from Harpers Ferry?

"It looks like the peninsula all over again," said Tom. "McClellan organized this army, trained it, and I'm afraid he doesn't want it to get hurt."

The remark was loaded. Tom had spoken without glancing at Wade, as if the latter were a soldier of shaded loyalties.

Wade took care to avoid criticism. "McClellan may just be biding his moment, maneuvering Lee onto open ground."

"He might be," muttered Tom, and allowed the subject of McClellan's abilities to lapse. He did not speak with Wade again before the regiment moved on at dawn.

The men walked stolidly through Turner's Gap, marching by companies, two hundred feet apart. Sporadic firing was heard at the vague and vast fringes, and the men seldom showed any interest in these skirmishes. It was the loose clatter of muskets, and not the heavy roar of a major engagement.

Then suddenly the Fifty-sixth emerged from the wooded east slope of the mountain and went down into a picturesque valley. On all sides neat farmhouses topped gently rolling hills. The light green squares of ripening corn, taller than a man, lay like quiltwork beside the darker patches of clover, the spangled orchards and kitchen gardens, and the russet-brown of plowed earth.

The names of the places he had come to and the various landmarks Wade learned later, and he never forgot them. The sturdy town was Sharpsburg; the lone white brick building, crowning an eminence to the north, was the Dunker Church. The slow-running creek was the Antietam.

What Wade and the men of the Fifty-sixth saw and could recognize instantly was the enemy. Lee had already collected some of his forces in Sharpsburg. Here on a rude peninsula, with the wiggling Potomac at his back and the steep-banked Antietam directly to his front, Lee had been tracked by Special Orders 191. And here he had turned to make his stand.

The Northern army deployed in its majestic might along the east ridges of the creek all morning. On the opposite shore, the Southerners arrayed, stretching lean their ranks to mirror the foe at all points and thwart a flanking attack. When the armies were in place, the front spread four miles from tip to tip.

Wade's thoughts flew across the Antietam to those

dauntless Reb fighters. Surely they needed all their courage as they beheld the blue troops of cavalry trotting into positions, the steely glint of artillery batteries unlimbering, the endless files of infantry massing to crumple them and trample them, and drown by the hair those who retreated to the Potomac.

At noon the Union artillery opened as though heralding a general assault. The Confederates did not retaliate. Their big guns waited ominously.

"They're savin' the heavy stuff for us infantry," brooded a bald-headed sergeant.

Off to the north there was a roll of drums. A bugle sang briefly, its notes shattered in air by a burst of shooting. Wade stared in the direction of the noises but could glimpse nothing beyond the Dunker Church, some two miles distant. An impenetrable curtain of woods, orchards, and farmhouses hid whatever was happening.

Impatience ruffled the Fifty-sixth. The men believed the decisive battle of the war was at hand. They were in a way eager to engage the Rebs. Frightened and longing for the climax of their fright, they wanted the battle over and done with.

The sun declined, and the noises on the right died out, except for lonely duels between pickets, and the order to advance was not issued. Instead, the Fifty-sixth shifted to the extreme left of the Union line. Fires being forbidden, the men ate their coffee dry, mixing the grinds with sugar between the palms of their hands. They slept that night on their guns.

They were awakened in the chilly blackness of predawn by the furious shelling of the Union artillery.

"It's startin'," said a sallow private, grimacing and kneading his hands steadily. "We'll be in for it soon."

As the sun rose and cast light over the Antietam, the sputtering of muskets swelled savagely. An all-out attack was being launched somewhere. To Wade and the men of the Fifty-sixth the fighters involved were phantoms in the wings. Their sector continued in mysterious quiet.

Some activity did for a short period break the eerie stillness in front of them. Around six o'clock a Rebel battery spotted a New York regiment in a cornfield northeast of Wade. Round balls lobbed across the Antietam, causing no casualties but forcing the regiment to retreat to a hollow. After this flurry, the sector reverted to its unnatural calm.

"I don't like it," said Tom. "It's too quiet."

The hillside facing theirs was bare of soldiers, though the youths knew the ground beyond their sight must be canalled with rifle pits and cannon entrenchments. In the gully of the Antietam, a triple-arched stone bridge stood almost directly below them.

"If we go for it," commented Tom at last, "it will be across that bridge." He stirred about uncomfortably. "I guess we're going, sooner or later, and before we do, I want to say I'm sorry about what I've been thinking. Afterward, I may not get the chance."

"You'll come through it," Wade assured him.

"I dunno," said Tom. "Anyway, I want to square myself with you. I've been thinking some hard thoughts the last couple of days."

"You've been thinking I'm more Reb than Yank? Forget it."

Tom poked his head above the crest of the knoll behind which they lay and studied the opposite shore. "Are they much different from us?" he asked gravely.

"Right now I guess they're just as scared."

"I mean ——"

"No, they're not much different," answered Wade. "I wish they were. It would be easier to kill them."

A sudden crackle of shooting brought half the regiment up to the knoll with the youths. Far below, a squad of Union soldiers edging through the trees had been discovered by the Confederates. The bluecoats were torn and routed by enfilade fire.

Twice more small detachments of infantry made sorties, feeling for a way to the bridge, and were cruelly repulsed. These failures added to the general dread that the Rebels, aware that a successful crossing would endanger their flank, had engineered ingenious, attack-proof fortifications.

About eleven o'clock a report circulated that General Burnside, commanding the corps which included the Fifty-sixth, had ignored General McClellan's order to storm across the bridge. A young private rose tremblingly to insist the report was correct. He had overheard, he claimed, General Burnside confide to an aide, "I will not send my men to be slaughtered!"

As if to bear up the truth of his quotation, the private lectured his audience on the observable Confederate practice of posting new troops. Units freshly arriving on the battlefield were sent to the conflict raging near the Dunker Church.

"They don't need any more troops opposite us," the private concluded, growing louder and shriller. "They got that bridge watched like a coon in a snake pit."

The ordeal of waiting terminated shortly after noon. The regiment moved under orders down a wooded slope to a path paralleling the creek. The men spoke not at all. Wade's mouth was dry as pine shavings.

An outbreak of shooting told of an assault by regiments closer to the bridge. Through the maze of locust trees Wade saw the hillside opposite fogging with artillery smoke. The fog was pierced everywhere by the red, rapier-like flames of muskets.

He could not see the bridge, but presently by an order he had not heard, the entire body of men was going for it on the run.

The Confederates across the creek, entrenched within accurate pistol range, laid down a withering fire. Men screamed and fell, but the regiment plunged on like a herd of rampaging steers.

Ahead now was the bridge, blistered by infantrymen. Over its back they dashed, and at its side they stood to the wall and doggedly pecked at the enemy. Upon its approaches companies choked in mobbed confusion. Shell and grape rained down, maiming and killing by the hundreds. The assault had become a stampede, a jumble of individual wrestling matches as men sought the protective furrows of the far bank.

An officer, conspicuous because he stood bravely planted, shouted at every passing company. He was signaling by holding one arm extended and the other circling toward it. He appeared to be directing men away from the bridge and farther up the creek. He was a pebble trying to divert a rapids. The men streamed by him.

A feather-light stinging ran along Wade's neck below the ear. He clapped a hand to the wound as he passed the officer. Then his mind went blank.

A shock of coldness revived him, and he discovered he was free of the turmoil around the bridge. He was clambering up a terrifically steep bank, snarling and baring his teeth like an animal.

He felt suddenly weighted down, soggy. His feet squished in his shoes; his hips and legs were drenched. A feeling of horror swept him. He believed himself bleeding to death. Drips slid down his arms and collected between his fingers.

He moaned and threw himself into a depression. He touched his soaked thighs and stared down at himself. Water! He began to laugh gleefully. It was *water!* He remembered the officer shouting . . . shouting about a ford. He had waded across!

The wound in his neck had stopped stinging. His body felt whole and sealed. He picked up his rifle and crawled forward.

The fighting on the Rebels' side of the Antietam whirled shapelessly. Everything was violent noises, everybody clumsy and bumping into things. The gray faces of the Rebs dissolved into smoke like sneering ghosts.

Wade held his fire till he saw a foe clearly. In this deliberateness he was singular. Soldiers shot as fast as they could pull the trigger and reload, as if a Southerner hid under every stone.

It was every man for himself. Through the uproar, officers waved their pistols and sabers and hollered "Fire low! Fire low!" alternating with, "Give it to 'em, boys!"

The precise whereabouts of the enemy was continually difficult to determine. Wade picked up the trail of knapsacks, overcoats, and blankets hurled down by the Union regiments farthest in advance. Above a ridge he spied a Reb in a knit cap.

Wade fired, aiming too quickly, and he knew he'd missed. A bullet sizzled nearby, and he hugged the ground.

Off to his right four soldiers and a lieutenant came at a charge. They seemed to have an objective, and so Wade attached himself to them. The group progressed fifty rods. Their legs gave out just as they encountered a nest of Rebel sharpshooters. Wade and the lieutenant survived by rolling downhill into a hollow.

A shell exploded, showering dirt on them. The lieutenant cringed and cursed. "We've got heavier artillery. We've murdered their gunners all along the line. But we can't get at them *here!*"

The lieutenant glowered at the sky and cursed again. He seemed outraged that the Rebs did not fight fairly. "They've got stone walls to duck behind and the woods to fall back into," he ranted. He popped a shot with his pistol, as though reproaching an enemy who didn't stand up in a nice level field and wage an honorable war.

The Rebs held them pinned down for what seemed like hours, until compelled to fall back before a wave of bluecoats. The spectacle of a general retreat brought a chorus of triumphant shouts.

"We're winning! We're winning!" rang out, spurring

terrified and exhausted men to leap up like fresh and eager reserves.

Wade ran, firing methodically. The barrel of his rifle heated till it boiled his hands. Sweat bore the grime of powder smudges into his eyes. But the current of victory flowed in him and lifted his weariness. The Rebs were retreating!

"Wade, over here!"

"Tom!"

Side by side once more, the two friends jogged along a road that led to an elevation formerly held by a Reb battery. From the vantage point of a disabled cannon and three dead cannoneers, they viewed a large segment of the battlefield.

The fighting had rolled up to its climax. Union artillery had got across the Antietam and was supporting troops who fought into the eastern suburbs of Sharpsburg. An aggressive push now against the desperate Rebs would turn the flank and send the Union forces free-wheeling across the Confederate rear. Lee's retreat to the Potomac would be cut off.

At this juncture, bluecoats charged from a cornfield to the south in number strong enough to clinch the day. The two youths whooped simultaneously.

Wade's cry died in his throat. The new troops were coming from the wrong direction. Impossible . . .

"How the —" gasped Tom. "Look behind them!"

More and more troops broke from the cover of the tall Indian corn. But they were not wearing blue uniforms! Like their comrades who were, they directed a slaughterous attack on the Union's exposed left flank.

Tom grasped the cause of the catastrophe nimbly. "Some of Jackson's men up from Harpers Ferry in stolen uniforms," he exclaimed.

The surprise attack decided the day. The Southern troops rallied, reformed, and beat back persistent Union charges. By nightfall the lines stabilized. Sharpsburg returned to Confederate possession. General Burnside's Northern brigades retired in a wide arc, the ends at the Antietam and the middle curving onto the hills overlooking the enemy.

"Why the devil did old Burnside delay so awful long this morning!" one soldier swore, loud enough for half the corps to hear. "Two hours! If we'd of attacked two hours earlier, we'd of bagged the whole dadblamed army and ended the war!"

No attempt was made to silence him, or the ripples of agreement that spread among the jury of weary men. The Fifty-sixth had advanced its position, but too many comrades had died to win a few hundred yards of farmland.

It was getting colder. A staff officer came through the area rounding up squads to bring in the wounded and dying.

Wade volunteered. He laid his rifle across his blanket roll, and walked out to where night pressed onto the mutilated fields.

*Chapter 13*

# Aftermath

NIGHT VEILED MUCH OF THE HORROR. IN THE MORNING MEN would turn from the sights and sicken at the odors; but now, as Wade and the squads of volunteers did their work, it was the noises which started a queasiness in the pit of the stomach.

From all corners of the battleground — from woods and rocks and fields, from gullies and breastworks and fences — the wounded cried out. The terrified ones shrieked, the brave ones pleaded brokenly for water.

Ambulance lanterns shed dim bubbles of light wherever soldiers lay thickest. A temporary truce, noddingly acknowledged by both sides, allowed Reb and Yank to mingle freely, and to gather their casualties without danger.

Members of both ambulance corps went out in full

force. Expertly they loaded men onto hand litters and transferred them to ambulances. A few of the vehicles were the new four-wheelers; most, however, had two wheels, and Wade sympathized with the pitiable wrecks of men, who, despite a bedding of hay, would be jolted and roughly tossed about.

Wade and the other volunteers acted as water-bearers and assisted in removing the most critically hurt. They fashioned rude litters from materials available. Fence gates, blankets, overcoats, and ladders sufficed in the race against daylight and the awakening of the cannons.

As he toiled, Wade became increasingly grateful for the intense darkness. It seemed that he had trod miles, and seldom did his feet step on bare ground for more than a yard or two. He tripped constantly on the spongy carpet of the dead.

Once he nearly lost his hold on the litter, and the soldier carrying the other end said sharply, "Baxter, you ought to have somebody tend to *you*. You're shakin' this boy like you got the malaria."

Wade mumbled an apology. Fatigue dragged at him; the wound which he'd suffered at the bridge had commenced to throb. When they had safely delivered their passenger, he proceeded to a field hospital.

He did not venture inside. The agonies of the hundreds laid in rows like fish reduced his own hurt to shameful insignificance. He sagged down and sipped from his canteen. Through the moans and sobbing grated the relentless screech of a saw.

Suddenly a lantern splashed light into his eyes. A voice behind the light exclaimed: "Well, I'll be danged. Hey, Bill, look here, will yuh."

The lantern lowered. Wade distinguished two Rebs standing over him.

The lantern swung sideways, as if the men behind it were examining his features. "Beats anythin' I ever seen."

"What does?" demanded Wade irritably.

"You," said the second Reb. "I got an idea we seen yuh in a Rebel uniform not long ago."

"Is that so?" Wade wove the straps of his canteen quickly about his fist. He could, if attacked, swing it like a ball and chain. He made no other move.

"What do yuh say, Bill? Ain't I right?"

The second Reb edged up and whistled. The musket under his arm flashed dully in the lantern light.

Except for the canteen, Wade was defenseless. If these two Rebs placed him in Harvey Hill's Confederate division, he'd have to fight or be taken prisoner. The informal truce did not protect a spy or deserter.

Bill snapped his fingers. "I got it, Ed," he said, his voice trailing off in amazement.

Wade gauged his chance of stunning Bill and then bolting for the Union lines. He carefully shifted his weight, trimming his balance for the dash.

Bill was whispering into Ed's ear. Wade heard the last words, after Ed snorted for Bill to speak up: ". . . over by the little white church, up agin the fence."

"Danged iffen it ain't so!" asserted Ed.

The two Rebs shuffled apart. They appeared troubled. Finally Ed said, "You got a twin brother with us, Yank?"

Wade had begun to shake his head when understanding caught onto him in a subtle tingle, and shot into his brain. "How is he?"

"He's dead, Yank."

"Can you lead me to him?"

"I reckon yuh got a right t' see he's done decent. Come on."

They came to a log fence manned by a dozen Confederates whose weapons had already been pried from their stiffly resisting fingers.

Bill raised the lantern by an officer.

The face was clean-shaven, unbloodied. The expression was that of a youth who had fallen peacefully asleep. For the first time Wade saw how young and unmenacing Roger Bragg really was, in spite of the fierce scar which slanted the length of his cheek.

Wade felt he must say something, but he could find no phrase to utter his sorrow. In the dark and deathflung night, it was as if they had been true twins, of one mother and one father, not fate-driven enemies. Their lives had touched and interwoven, a single thread in the ugly tapestry of war. Now the deadly hide-and-seek between them was over, and he would never know Roger Bragg in peace and gladness.

"I wish I might have heard your laughter," Wade thought.

He turned and walked slowly back to the Union lines. The questioning calls of the two Rebs he ignored, for he was remembering how he had curled in a hogshead and ripped Roger Bragg's cheek with his shot.

He erased the picture from his memory. As he went across the immense carpet of dead, he ached with the great weariness of despair. There seemed nothing in war and soldiering worthy of not being forgotten.

In the morning Lee patched his torn and battered division, shortened his front, and stood ready to repel attack.

The groggy Northern giant did not attack; it had had enough. That night, under a spray of artillery, the Southerners limped across the Potomac and onto Virginia soil. Lee had saved the Confederate army.

The battle of Antietam, the most destructive ever fought till then on the American continent, was over. It had strewn the ground with eleven thousand Southerners and twelve thousand Northerners, dead and wounded.

Both sides claimed victory, because the numbers slaughtered could not be justified in defeat. The evidence favored the North; the invasion by Lee had been repulsed, and the Union soldiers had at last seen the Rebs show their backs.

Far away in Washington, where the dead were not seen, Abraham Lincoln viewed the halting of Lee as the victory he so fervently desired. Five days later he warned the Southern states that unless they returned to the Union their slaves would be declared free.

The war had grown in purpose. Henceforth it was fought not only to preserve the Union, but as a crusade to abolish slavery. The first note of the death knell tolled for the Confederacy.

The Emancipation Proclamation was formally issued on January 1, 1863, and the news reached the Fifty-sixth a day later. Wade heard it from Tom Watson.

He was sitting on a rock and nibbling a soggy wheat biscuit when Tom came slogging through the thunderstorm and told him. They sat together, mud-splattered, chilled, soaked to the skin, and they grinned like hunters eating their kill before a cozy fire.

"It was you and Special Orders No. 191 that did it," exulted Tom.

Right there Wade had all of his reward. In the apparatus of the emancipation he had simply helped turn one wheel, but that wheel had been a vital one. It turned, and it set all men free. A sudden, bursting glow of pride suffused him.

He broke off half the biscuit and gave it to Tom; Tom raised his half in a toast.

"To the end of the war."

"To a long and happy life," responded Wade.

It came to pass that Wade had his wish, and many moments of the years thereafter were suffused with that golden warmth of pride. A quarter century later, still tall and straight, he traveled with his family to see Luke's oldest boy graduate from Hampton Institute in Virginia. And later, much later, he placed his gnarled hand on his wife's as together they cut their fiftieth wedding cake, an elaborate, snowy white structure of twenty layers.

There were these moments and more, but none filled him with the pride of that cold, rainy day when he was young and strong and he sat on a rock and shared a wheat biscuit with Tom.

## Date Due